The Mystery of the Coins

The MYSTERY of the COINS

Written and Illustrated by
CHAYA M. BURSTEIN

UAHC Press · New York, New York

To Rivka and Avishai,
our family's newest links
to the future

I'm very grateful for the resources of the fine libraries
of Haifa University and the Museum of the Diaspora in Israel
which I used extensively

Library of Congress Cataloging-in-Publication Data
Burstein, Chaya M.
The mystery of the coins / written and illustrated by Chaya Burstein.
      p.   cm.
Summary: Two children and their grandmother, with the help of a
book about coins and a Jewish history book, explore the stories
behind the coins found in a dead man's trunk.
ISBN 0–8074–0350–4
1. Jews—History—Juvenile fiction.   [1. Jews—History—Fiction.
2. Jews—Fiction.   3. Mystery and detective stories.]   I. Title.
PZ7.B94553My   1988
[Fic]—dc19   87–24867   CIP
AC

Dear Reader,

To solve this strange mystery, Jamie, Sarah, their grandmother—and you—must uncover a dead man's secret. It won't be easy. You will find clues that go back through 3,400 years of Jewish history. Each clue has a story to tell about its own people, time, and place.

With the help of a book about coins and a book of Jewish history, Jamie, Sarah, and Grandmother guess at the story behind each clue. But you, the reader, won't have to guess. The stories are right here waiting for you.

Who will find out more about the 3,400-year journey of the Jewish people—you or the three detectives in the book? And who will be the first to solve the mystery of the coins?

Contents

Introduction

Uncle Otto's Trunk

On the day of Grandma's yard sale, Jamie and Sarah found a dusty, wooden trunk in the basement.

"Achoo," sneezed Jamie, as the dust tickled his nose. "This trunk must be a million years old."

"Watch out; maybe there's a genie inside," Sarah giggled. She loved to make up stories.

"Grandma, do you want this trunk?" Jamie yelled.

Grandma peered down. "Oh, my goodness—Uncle Otto's trunk!" She clapped her hand to her cheek. "It's been down there for years and years. I forgot all about it."

"Should we bring it up for the yard sale?"

"Why not!" said Grandma. She turned away, then quickly turned back. "No, maybe not . . . I promised. . . ."

"Promised what?" Sarah perked up. She looked curiously at the old trunk.

"But it's so many years," Grandma seemed to be arguing with herself. "If it was important, somebody would've come for it."

"For what? What's important?" Sarah asked eagerly.

"Never mind. It's a long story." Grandma sighed and shook her head. "Bring it up, children. And hurry—we have to sell everything quickly before the rain starts. The clouds are getting blacker and blacker."

Jamie and Sarah carried the trunk up and dropped it on the grass.

"What goodies do you have in there?" asked Mrs. Stein, Grandma's next-door neighbor. She hurried over to look, pulling four-year-old Jennifer along.

"Some old things my Uncle Otto left," said Grandma. She lifted the

1

lid and took out a few books and a long leather coat, moldy green at the edges. Yellowing towels and shirts filled the bottom.

"Some genie!" Jamie poked Sarah. "It's all junk."

"Junk," sniffed Mrs. Stein. "But still . . ." she stepped back to look at the trunk's carved wooden sides, "if I scrubbed it well and painted it red, it would look very nice in Jennifer's playroom. What do you think?"

"Playroom?" Grandma looked uncomfortable. She glanced over the cluttered lawn, saw an old laundry hamper, and suggested, "How about this wicker basket? It's perfect for a playroom."

Sarah poked Jamie back. "There's something weird about that trunk. Grandma really doesn't want to sell it," she whispered. "We have to get rid of Mrs. Stein."

"No, I like the trunk better than the basket. I could glue flower decals on it to jazz it up," Mrs. Stein said, opening her purse. "How much do you want?"

"I wouldn't want that trunk in *my* playroom," Sarah said loudly. "It's a million years old, and it's probably haunted." She pulled the lid down and it screeched as if in pain. "See!"

"Ooooooo," Jamie moaned and flapped his arms over the dusty lid. The wind was beginning to moan through the yard too, flapping the yard-sale sign.

"Don't get it, Mommy. It's haunted," Jennifer wailed, tugging at her mother's arm.

"Don't be silly," Mrs. Stein snapped, but she looked doubtful and stopped fishing for her wallet. Just then there was a low rumble of thunder, followed by huge, splattering drops of rain.

Mrs. Stein scooped up Jennifer, waved, and raced for home. Grandma plunked a paper bag on her head to protect her hairdo and yelled, "Quick, Jamie, Sarah, help me pull everything into the garage."

They raced back and forth, carrying lamps, books, tricycles, dishes, and the old trunk. At last they finished and came dripping into Grandma's warm kitchen.

"Take off your shoes and socks," she ordered. "Then we'll have hot cocoa and oatmeal cookies so we shouldn't catch cold."

"Then will you tell us about Uncle Otto's trunk?" Sarah asked.

*   *   *

"Uncle Otto, may he rest in peace, came to our house from Europe after the war," Grandma told them. "He wasn't really my uncle. He and

another boy were my father's best friends. The three boys grew up together in Russia, in the town of Hashvata, but later went their separate ways."

"Hash–who?" asked Jamie.

"God bless you!" Sarah laughed.

Grandma didn't even smile. She went on with her story earnestly. "Uncle Otto was a tall, thin, quiet man who coughed a great deal. He brought only one thing with him—the wooden trunk. He carried it into the guest room himself and kept it there."

"What country did he come from?" Jamie asked. He had just finished studying World War Two in social studies and he could rattle off the names of all the countries of Europe.

"After leaving Hashvata, he went to Czechoslovakia," said Grandma. "There his whole family was killed in the Holocaust. Only Uncle Otto and a daughter survived. My father told me that the daughter had gone to Palestine before the war, but Uncle Otto never talked about her or about the war or the Nazis . . . not until the very end."

"Is that when he told you about the trunk—at the very end?" Sarah asked.

"No. He never said anything about the trunk. He became even more silent as he grew more ill. Finally we took him to the hospital. Just a few days before he died, he began to talk deliriously. He didn't make any sense at all—just kept shouting, 'It's blood money! Give it back! Give it to the synagogue! I don't want it!'

"Grandpa and I asked him, 'Give *what* back? What money? You don't have any money, Uncle Otto.' But he wouldn't listen. He kept crying, 'Give it back! It's blood money—Jewish blood money!'

"We had to calm him down, so we finally said, 'All right, Uncle Otto. Whatever it is, we'll find it and give it back. We promise. Don't worry.' After that he just lay back quietly and closed his eyes. Three days later he died."

"Poor, lonely Uncle Otto." Sarah said.

"But what was he talking about? What's blood money?" Jamie asked.

Grandma sighed and shook her head. "I don't know. After the funeral we searched Uncle Otto's trunk. It contained only the things you saw today. There was nothing of any value. So Grandpa put the trunk down in the basement. We thought somebody might know Uncle Otto's secret and would come for the trunk. But it's been so many years. Nobody ever came. Today I said to myself, 'Enough already; it's time to sell the trunk.' "

"But, Grandma, you promised!" Sarah said.

"I know, I know." Grandma sighed again. "All right. Finish your cocoa; then we'll put it back in the basement. After all, how much room does it take?"

Jamie and Sarah ate a few more cookies; then they grabbed the leather handles and carried the trunk to the cellar door.

"Be careful of the steps," Grandma warned.

They tipped it slowly down onto the first step. Suddenly one of the hardened leather handles tore loose. The trunk slid from their hands and went bumping, scraping, and grinding down the steps. With a crash it smashed open against the brick furnace wall at the bottom.

A cloud of dust rose up the stairwell.

"Oh, wow!" Jamie's shocked voice broke the silence. "That's the end of Uncle Otto's trunk." But, as he and Sarah peered down through the dust, they heard a new sound—a tiny, tinkling sound of small objects spilling onto the concrete basement floor.

They scrambled down and dropped to their knees beside the trunk.

Grandma hurried close behind, crying, "Watch out for splinters!"

"Look, there are two bottoms!" Jamie yelled, pointing inside the trunk to a narrow space filled with thick, soft fabric and small, black discs.

"What *is* this stuff, Grandma?"

Grandma pulled her glasses out of her apron pocket, knelt in the dust, and lifted one of the discs. She turned it slowly in her hand. "It looks like money," she said quietly.

"Uncle Otto's blood money," Sarah whispered.

* * *

The next day, after school, Jamie and Sarah skipped soccer practice and rode their bikes straight to the library.

"Got a new hobby?" asked the librarian as she stamped the library card for a large book called *Coins of the World*.

Sarah and Jamie exchanged a private grin. If she only knew.

Grandma was waiting for them. On the table next to their milk and graham crackers were a new notebook, two sharp pencils, a magnifying glass, a Jewish history book, and a mixing bowl filled with the strange coins.

"First of all, eat something," said Grandma.

Jamie started dunking crackers into his milk when he noticed the history book. "What's *that* for?" he asked, wrinkling up his nose. "It looks like school."

"*That* is to help us solve Uncle Otto's secret," said Grandma. "I think these may be very old Jewish coins because Uncle Otto called them 'Jewish blood money.' If I'm right, we'll need the coin book and the Jewish history book to help us discover the mystery of these coins."

"The—Mystery—of—the—Blood—Money," Jamie growled in his deepest "monster" voice.

"Stop kidding around, Jamie. We have a real mystery to solve," said Sarah. "Let's start!"

CHAPTER
1

"Some of the coins have bits of tape with numbers," said Grandma. "We'll pull out all the numbered coins and identify them."

Eager fingers dug into the pile. Soon fourteen coins were lined up on the table. There were also two black, oddly-shaped objects, labeled "One" and "Two."

"They're not coins. They're junk," said Jamie scornfully.

"Numbers One and Two must be important," Grandma said. "Look in the first few pages of the coin book, Jamie. Sarah, you draw a picture of each piece in the notebook. I'll clean them off."

The kitchen became very quiet. Sarah drew, Jamie turned pages, and Grandma rubbed. Suddenly they all yelled at the same time.

"Number Two is a piece of silver bracelet," cried Grandma.

"Number One is a tiny animal head," Sarah yelled.

"They're not junk!" Jamie cried. "Listen to what the book says."

Gold and silver were used as a means of exchange long before the first coins were struck. Merchants weighed bits of jewelry or other objects made of precious metals to establish their value and then used them in buying and selling merchandise.

A hoard of such objects, including the head of a horse, was found in the tell of ancient Jericho in the Jordan Valley at a level dating to 1500 B.C.E. The design of the horse's head (see illustration) suggests Egyptian influence.

Sarah leaned over Jamie's shoulder to see the illustration. "It looks exactly like our Number One," she said.

Grandma raced through the first few chapters of the history book. "Aha!" she said. "Fifteen hundred B.C.E. was a busy time in Jewish history. Moses was leading the tribes of Israel through the desert from Egypt to the Land of Israel. They started out as a frightened bunch of slaves, but, by the time they reached Jericho, they had become a brave, free people."

Sarah touched the tiny mouth of the horse. "Were you carried through the desert by a Jewish boy or girl? I wish you could tell us."

The Golden-Headed Horse

Sinai, 1500 B.C.E.

"Give it back. It's not yours! My friend Shishak gave it to me in Egypt." Rafi ran back and forth between his older brother, Binyamin, and his friend Menashe, and then on to Paltiel, as the three bigger boys threw Rafi's small toy horse over his head.

"You'll break it," he shrieked, as Paltiel caught it just before it hit the ground. The flinty desert soil wouldn't be easy on the pointed, golden ears and wooden body of the little horse.

"Come and get it, Rafi," Menashe teased, holding the little horse out to him. And then, as Rafi came hopefully, Menashe tossed it to Rafi's brother.

Binyamin caught it neatly with one hand. "All right, Rafi," he said, "you can have it if you promise not to follow us. We have important things to do."

"What are you going to do?"

"We're going scouting. Moses is going to send out scouts to see if the tribes can move up into the Promised Land. So we decided we would look around too. But you're too little. You'd slow us down. Go back to the tent and play with your horse."

"I don't want to. Mama and Papa are fighting again. This morning Papa hollered, 'We should've stayed in Egypt, like I told you. That Moses is going to get us all killed.' And Mama hollered back that Papa had the courage of a chicken. And then Papa . . ."

"They're scared," Binyamin said shortly. He turned away, calling, "Remember, don't follow us."

The three twelve-year-olds marched off, taking long strides like scouts, and disappeared into the narrow valley, the wadi, beside the campground of the tribe of Dan.

"I don't care what Binyamin says," Rafi grumbled to the little horse. "We're not going back to the tent. But I know how we can fool the big kids." His eyes sparkled gleefully. "We'll climb the hill at the side of the wadi and spy on them."

Rafi made a whinnying noise, as if his horse were answering him. Then he galloped across the dusty plain of the campsite and started to climb the hot, crumbly rock of the hill behind the camp.

Halfway up, a ledge jutted out. Rafi scrambled up over the edge on his stomach. When he straightened up, he nearly tumbled down the slope in surprise.

A man was sitting cross-legged in the shade at the back of the ledge—a square-shouldered man with a thick, gray beard and a crisscross of worry wrinkles around his eyes.

"Excuse me," Rafi mumbled and started to edge down.

"St-t-tay," said the man, "unless you're g-going t-to cry and c-complain like the others."

"I won't," Rafi promised, and he sat down.

For a while, he watched a lizard sunning itself, and then he remembered about the scouts. He leaned forward and squinted down into the wadi. But he could see only a green fuzz of bushes. Nothing moved. "I'm some spy," he thought. "Might as well go down."

Just then the man sighed. "P-people are n-never s-satisfied. I-I get so tired of h-hearing them cry and c-complain," he said.

Rafi nodded. "My mother and father complain a lot too. That's why I came up here instead of going back to the tent."

"Why do they c-complain?"

"Binyamin, my brother, says it's because they're scared of the desert. My father thinks we were safer in Egypt, even though we were slaves."

"B-but we're safe here!" The man waved his arms at the great semicircle of jagged, gray mountains. "God is here all around us, l-leading us and p-protecting us."

"Where?" Rafi asked.

"Everywhere. Most of the t-time we can't see or even t-touch God. It's not easy, l-like t-touching your little horse or a pagan idol. But we know that God is with us because of what God does."

"Binyamin, my brother, isn't scared. He's very brave, and he believes in God and trusts Moses," Rafi said proudly. "Today, he and Paltiel and Menashe are helping Moses do some scouting. I wanted to go too, but they wouldn't let me. They're down there in that wadi." He pointed.

"Are they?" The worry wrinkles deepened and turned up into a wide smile. "Moses is l-lucky to have their help." Then the man grew serious again. "Scouting is dangerous. I hope your brother knows about p-poisonous s-snakes and s-scorpions and about flash floods and such things."

Rafi squeezed his horse tightly and worried. He didn't know whether Binyamin knew about such things—whatever they were.

For a minute the man's eyes looked far, far away. "I was a shepherd in the d-desert once," he said, "and I learned how to d-deal with s-snakebites and other dangers." He pointed to the thick walking stick that lay on the ledge between them. "Once, not too long ago, this s-stick was a h-hissing, wriggling s-snake!"

Rafi jumped and backed away.

"B-but that's another story." The man quickly changed the subject. "If you want to go s-scouting with your brother, you need to know how to care for snakebites."

"Uh, uh—not me." Rafi shook his head. "I'm just a kid."

"The desert is a d-dangerous place. You may get into t-trouble when there are no grownups nearby to help you. Or the grownups may not know what to do. Remember, in a place where there are no adults you must try to be the adult . . . even though you're a k-kid. Now listen closely."

The man dipped his finger in the earth and made two dots on Rafi's arm. "P-pretend a s-snake just bit your friend." He pulled out a small knife and drew the edge lightly between the two dots. "You must c-cut across the bite hard enough to make it bleed. Then s-suck out the blood t-to draw out the venom. Don't swallow. Spit out the blood and s-suck again. And while you're doing that you pray for God's help with all your h-heart and all your m-might."

Rafi nodded. Staring at the two dots and at the sharp knife was giving him a rocking feeling in the stomach . . . like riding a camel.

"Remember, you must t-think of what to do, then act quickly, and p-pray for God's help."

"Think, act quickly, and pray for God's help," Rafi repeated.

The man put the knife away, hunted in his robe, and pulled out a handful of slightly sandy dates. "Have some," he said.

They sat side by side, eating dates, and watching the great, gray mountain opposite them—Mount Sinai—turn pink in the late afternoon light.

"I have to get back," the man said after a while. "P-people will be waiting for me."

"I'll go and meet Binyamin and the others. I'll tell them what you said, even if they make fun of me," said Rafi.

At the bottom of the hill, before they parted, the man clapped Rafi on the back. "D-don't you be afraid. We'll g-get there," he said. "We'll get to the l-land that God promised to us. Have faith in God and in yourself."

The man smiled, and Rafi smiled back. Suddenly Rafi felt strong and very happy. He started down into the wadi, singing to himself—until he heard a clatter of feet and hoarse shouting. A moment later Paltiel sprang up the wadi wall and flew past, running toward the camp, yelling, "Binyamin is hurt!"

Rafi slid to the wadi floor, scratching his legs on thorns and rocks, and then he raced along the bottom with his heart thumping with fear. Soon he saw Menashe standing alone. No, not alone, he was leaning over Binyamin, who lay on the ground.

"What happened?" Rafi gasped.

"A big bug with claws and a long tail . . . came out from between the rocks. I think it bit Binyamin's leg. He yelled and sat down . . . and then he got a funny look on his face and fell flat." Menashe began to cry. "I don't know what to do," he sobbed.

Rafi squatted beside his brother. There was a red, swollen mark on his ankle. What did the man say—think, act quickly, pray—cut, suck, spit, pray, pray, pray! His head was a jumble. But there was no time to be jumbled. He pulled out the little horse, pressed one pointy ear into the bite and drew it hard across until red blood welled up.

"Stop! What do you think you're doing?" Menashe was pulling fearfully at his belt. But Rafi was down on his hands and knees, with his mouth to the wound, sucking, spitting, sucking, spitting, and praying with all his might.

*   *   *

"How did you know what to do?" Binyamin asked weakly, days later, when the boys were gathered in the tent around his sleeping mat.

"Promise not to laugh, all right?" Rafi asked.

"Promise."

"There was this man on the mountain. He stuttered and had a gray beard, and he had a stick that was once a snake! We talked about God and snakes, and about you. And he said a strange thing. He said that in a place where there are no adults I have to try to be the adult, and that I should think and act quickly and pray to God. So that's what I did!"

For once Paltiel and Menashe didn't make fun of Rafi. They didn't say a word. They just stared.

Binyamin repeated, "He stuttered, he had a gray beard, and he had a stick that was once a snake!" He looked at Rafi with such wide-eyed respect that Rafi had to turn around to be sure his brother wasn't looking at somebody else.

"Rafi, you can come scouting with us whenever you want to," Binyamin said fervently.

CHAPTER
2

"This next paragraph in the coin book explains the bit of silver bracelet," said Jamie.

MEHUTAN HOARD, c. 1000 B.C.E.
The Mehutan Hoard, found in the Judean Desert near Jerusalem, dates to about 1000 B.C.E. It contains many fragments of silver jewelry which were probably used like money for buying and selling goods in the centuries before the development of coins.

"One thousand B.C.E.," said Grandma, leafing through the history book. "In 1000 B.C.E. the Jewish people were united and prosperous under King Solomon. They had just finished building the First Holy Temple in Jerusalem. People came to the Temple to worship God, bring sacrifices, and celebrate together during the harvest holidays of Pesach, Shavuot, and Sukot."

"The bit of bracelet must have been used for money in Jerusalem," Jamie suggested.

"But, before it was broken, it was somebody's beautiful bracelet," said Sarah. "Maybe King Solomon gave it to a princess."

"A little thing like that! It's more likely a shepherd boy gave it to a shepherd girl," Jamie laughed.

12

Trouble at the Temple

Judea, c. 1000 B.C.E.

The first time Sarah picked up a reed and blew into it, her father patted her black curls and said, "Very nice, little one, but some day we'll take you to the Holy Temple to hear the Levites play. That's real music!"

When she cut holes in the reed and began to play melodies, her older brother, who couldn't even whistle, said, "Not bad for a girl, but wait till you hear the music of the Levites at the Temple."

Sarah played all day while her sheep and goats grazed on the hillsides among the olive trees. Soon her flute could coo like a dove and wail like the afternoon wind. The sleepy lizards raised their heads, and the baby goats stopped to listen. When she came piping into the village, bringing the flock home, Simon the fool would smile and tap his foot.

The townspeople said, "Sarah plays the flute like young David played to cheer King Saul. Her music can make a sick person healthy."

"Nonsense," said Sarah's mother, worried that jealous, evil spirits might be listening. "Sarah is just a simple shepherd girl who plays with reeds. Only the music of the Levites can heal the sick."

Sarah blushed at the praise. "Someday, some wonderful day, I'm going to hear the Levites play," she told her goats and sheep. She kicked her brown legs and danced joyfully around the meadow as she thought about it. "The Levites don't play simple shepherd music. They play magical, heavenly music that opens the sky and reaches up to the great, golden throne of God."

One evening her mother took down the big, ivory comb and began to pull it through Sarah's mop of hair.

"Ooooch—ouch!" Sarah tried to jump away.

"Hold still," said her mother. "It's time to fix your hair and scrub the donkey dung from under your toenails. You have to look like a proper young woman because we are taking you to Jerusalem at Sukot. And while we're there we'll find a bridegroom for you."

"Ouch!" Sarah yelped. "I don't need a bridegroom!" Then she stopped jumping. "Where did you say we were going?" she asked.

"To Jerusalem, to the Holy Temple."

"Then we'll hear the Levites play!" Sarah shouted.

"We'll pray and bring gifts to God; Papa and I will take a look at the bridegroom we have in mind; and we'll hear the Levites play," her mother said as she yanked at the tangles in Sarah's hair.

When the moon was almost full, during the Hebrew month of Kislev, Sarah's family and other villagers loaded their oxen and donkeys with harvest for the priests and the Temple, tied flowers around their animals' necks, and happily made their way along the mountain trails to Jerusalem. More and more pilgrims joined them as they walked until, at the gates of the city, they were part of a great, shoving, singing, laughing crowd. Sarah held onto her donkey's tail to keep from being swept away as they made their way to the pilgrims' campground. "I didn't think there were so many people in the world," she marveled uneasily.

Early the next morning, dressed up in her new sandals and robe, Sarah started walking through the city with her mother, going up toward the Temple courtyard. Her neck ached from turning to see the new sights. Unlike her dusty village, Jerusalem was all stone. There were hard cobblestones below and stone city walls towering above. Far ahead she could see the rosy, stone walls of the Temple, and close by stood King Solomon's marble palace. The streets were already crowded with pilgrims and with peddlers selling sweet rolls, fruits, pigeons, and lulavim and etrogim for the holiday.

Somebody stepped on her foot, making her tight sandals feel even tighter. Her new, woolen robe itched. Her nose was filled with the smells of perfumes, sweat, herbs, and smoking meat. Only the flute tucked in her belt felt friendly and familiar.

"Mama, now can we go and hear the Levites?"

"Not yet. Look at the torch swallower." Her mother pulled her to the side. Sarah gaped as she watched a small, grinning man gulp down a great, orange flame. She was pulled a few steps further and saw a swaying, tongue-flicking snake rise out of a basket while his master played the flute. "I can do that," she thought excitedly, drawing out her flute. But her mother was already moving on to watch a pair of jugglers.

Suddenly a donkey carrying crates of pigeons bumped between them and knocked the flute from Sarah's hand. She flung herself to the ground, batted her head against legs and skirts, and snatched up the slim flute just before a big, hairy foot smashed it.

Sarah struggled back up into the daylight, red-faced and shaking, her braids coming apart. "I've had enough of Jerusalem," she gasped. "Mama, where are you?"

Her mother's strong, brown hand plucked her out of the crowd. "It's time to hear the Levites. Come. But fix your hair first. You're a mess. What will he think?"

"He?" Sarah asked. Then she remembered—the bridegroom. But she pushed that worry out of her head. She was going to hear the Levites, the sweet singers and musicians of Israel. She flew up the Temple steps ahead of her mother, through the carved gates into the women's courtyard. A tower of smoke rose into the air before them. The priests standing on top of the high, brass altar in the inner courtyard were offering sacrifices. Other priests were washing their hands in a huge, bronze basin that was three times as large as the well in Sarah's village and was held on the backs of twelve iron oxen. Soon the Levites would add their gift of music for God and God's people.

Sarah's mother edged closer to the inner court. Up on her tiptoes, behind a fat lady in a polka-dotted robe, Sarah could see the top of the great altar and the small figures of the priests. Then the lady moved, and she could see only polka dots.

"I can't see," she whispered.

"Listen!" her mother whispered back excitedly. "The priests have raised their arms."

The crowd hushed as a great clang filled the air. It echoed against the altar and against the carved, gold-covered walls, and then slowly it faded to a hum. Music of harps and lyres began to ripple over the sunny courtyard. The rippling grew louder and louder until it pounded like the stormy waves of Lake Kinneret in midwinter. Then, suddenly, whistles shrilled from each side of the altar, stabbing through the waves of music. Just as Sarah was about to clap her hands to her ears, the whistling began to fade, and the pounding of the harps and lyres softened. Playful, piping flute sounds danced lightly and happily above them.

Sarah forgot the fat lady. She forgot to be afraid of the crowds or worry about a bridegroom. She could think only of the music. These were the sweetest sounds she had ever heard. They were rising straight into the sky along with the smoke of the sacrifices—right to God. She raised her flute. She wanted to make sweet music for God too.

"No!" Sarah heard her mother's urgent whisper and felt a firm hand on her arm. "Put the flute away!"

"Why?" Sarah asked.

"Sssssshhhhh," the fat lady hissed, turning around and glaring at her.

"Ssshh," whispered the people all around her.

Tears of disappointment filled Sarah's eyes, and she tucked the flute back into her belt.

*   *   *

The full moon was rising over the hills of Jerusalem when Sarah and her mother started down the hill to the campsite. Cooking fires flickered around them. A boy pounded a clay drum, and the pilgrims sang as they prepared the evening meal.

Sarah's fingers itched at the sound of the music. But again she felt her mother's hand. "Sarah, you mustn't play your flute in public. You must be modest and polite. Papa and I have spoken to the parents of a fine boy. They'll be watching you."

"I don't know how to be modest and polite," Sarah cried. "I just know how to make music and take care of my flock. I'm a village girl." The tears filled her eyes again. "I want to go home," she thought. "I heard the Levites and they made me very happy, but now I want to go home."

"Help, help!" Wild yells from down the hill shocked Sarah out of her misery. A moment later a gaunt man came crashing up through the bushes, clutching a thick branch. A woman stumbled close behind.

"Thieves, murderers," the man yelled. "Help me, help—they're killing me!" He swung the branch about him, plunged through a cooking fire and scattered people in all directions.

"Stop him," wailed the woman. "There's a devil in him."

The man tripped and fell just as he reached Sarah. "Help, save me!" he cried hoarsely. The branch fell from his hands, and he covered his eyes with his fists and rolled back and forth at her feet.

"My poor husband," the woman sobbed. "He's a farmer, quiet as a dove. But here in Jerusalem he changed. An evil spirit got into him."

An evil spirit! At those frightening words women snatched up their children, and everybody began to back away. Sarah's mother touched her amulet for protection and tried to pull Sarah away too. But the girl would not budge.

"There's no devil in him," she thought. "He's just frightened, like me." She dropped to her knees beside the struggling man. A young man in a striped robe came out of the crowd and knelt too.

"Hold him, please," said Sarah. "I can help him."

Sarah pulled out her flute and closed her eyes. She forgot the crowded campsite and thought of the flowers that cover the Judean hills in the spring. Then she began to play. She played the whisper of the breeze in the thick leaves of the fig trees and the baa of new lambs. She played the slow songs shepherds sing to their flocks on hot afternoons and the sound of the quick patter of rain on thirsty earth.

As she played, the man's breathing grew quieter.

Her flute sounds rose like the whirring of birds through the olive groves and finally faded into sleepy, twilight nesting sounds.

When she opened her eyes, the man was asleep. She looked around and found everybody watching her. "Oh, no," she groaned, "now Mama will be angry, and the boy's parents will think I'm awful. I spoiled everything." She jumped up, pulled her scarf over her face, and ran off into the stubbly field.

From the Temple Mount she heard the sounds of trumpets and singing. But inside her head she was hearing, "His parents will be watching . . .

be modest . . . polite." She ran further and further, wishing she could run all the way home.

Suddenly somebody caught her shoulder and spun her around. In the moonlight she saw a broad-shouldered boy in a crumpled, striped robe. He was breathing hard from running.

"Sarah?" he asked.

"I'm Sarah. And you're the one who helped me."

He nodded. "I thought I'd never catch you. I . . . I . . . ." he stopped, scratched his head, embarrassed, and finally blurted, "I'm Gidon. Your parents spoke to my parents. . . ."

Sarah clapped her hand to her cheek. "So you're the fine young man. It's because of you that I got into trouble!" She wasn't upset any more—she was indignant. "Well I can't be modest and polite. I had to help that man. He's a villager like me, and he was scared."

"I'm a villager too," said Gidon. "See?" He held out his broad, hard hands. "You were wonderful. You play just like the Levites."

Sarah turned red.

"Even better," he added.

He smiled shyly. Sarah smiled too. "I like him," she thought with surprise.

They stared at each other and down at the ground, not knowing what to say next. "I have to go back," Sarah said finally.

"Wait," said Gidon. "We may not see each other for a long time. My family is going home tomorrow." He slipped a silver bracelet off his wrist. "Please take this so you won't forget me."

Sarah's black eyes sparkled, and she grinned happily as she took the bracelet. "I'll think of you whenever I play the flute," she said.

CHAPTER
3

"Here's our first real coin," Jamie said, "Number Three, yellowish with dirty spots."

Grandma rubbed for a few seconds. The coin began to gleam in the afternoon sun that lit the kitchen. "It's gold," she announced, "and there's a design on it."

Sarah and Jamie both leaned over the magnifying glass. "Ouch!" they yelled as they bumped heads.

"You're the looker-upper so you have to let me examine," Sarah yelled, rubbing her head.

"Examining is more fun. Looking-up is hard."

Grandma shook her finger at them. "No fighting. We're too busy. You'll take turns. Next time Jamie will examine."

"I see a tiger or a lion's head on the left and a funny-looking thing with ears on the right," said Sarah slowly.

As Sarah started to draw, Jamie moved his finger slowly down the pages of the coin book. On page six, he yelled, "Got it!" and began to read aloud.

GOLD STATER, c. 540 B.C.E.
This coin, minted by King Croesus of Lydia, is among the first coins ever to be minted. It shows a lion, the symbol of Lydia, attacking a bull. After the conquest of Lydia by Cyrus, king of Persia, in 546 B.C.E., these coins began  to be used in Babylonia and throughout the Persian Empire.

Grandma the historian found 540 B.C.E. in her book. "In the sixth century B.C.E., which means the years between 600 and 500 Before the Common Era, the Jews of Judea were conquered and dragged off to Babylonia as captives. Later King Cyrus of Persia conquered the Babylonians and let the Jews go home," she told them.

"Good ol' Cyrus," Jamie said.

"But maybe some of the Jews didn't want to go back," Sarah said. "The kids had to leave their friends, and the grownups had to leave their jobs and houses. . . ."

"You get the goofiest ideas, Sarah. Of course they'd want to go back. They were going home," Jamie argued.

But Sarah shook her head stubbornly. "I wish the gold stater could tell us," she said.

Joseph the Carver

Babylonia, c. 540 B.C.E.

Tap, tap, tap. Joseph's chisel bit into the odd-shaped stone on the work table. The gray chips flew, and the stone slowly became a rough, crouching lion. The boy brushed the curly, black hair from his eyes and bent to look carefully at his work. Here was the head and the heavy mane; here, the big, bunched-up shoulders; here, the folded legs. Good! Joseph began to cut more slowly, humming happily under his breath. He loved the feel of the chisel, and he loved to carve. It was as if he were freeing a living creature from the rock.

Zayyid, the owner of the gem shop where Joseph worked, came up softly behind him and watched. He smiled and rubbed his hands together. "This boy is a treasure," he thought. "At fourteen he's already the best and fastest carver in the shop. Maybe the best in Babylonia. Our new king, Cyrus, will want plenty of seals and statues and amulets. The boy will serve me well.

"Joseph," he said, "Put aside the lion. I have a rush job here—a chunk of unflawed alabaster sent by the king's chief scribe. He wants a gazelle. Can you do it?"

Joseph studied the white stone for a moment. Then he knelt and, with a stick, scratched a slim, leaping shape on the earthen floor.

Zayyid nodded. "You have good hands. Someday you'll carve gemstones for the crown of the great god Marduk."

Joseph blushed. "Marduk is not my god," he stammered. "I am a Jew."

"Jew or Babylonian, it makes no difference. We all belong to Marduk," Zayyid replied. He pushed aside the lion. "Now get to work and make that gazelle leap from the alabaster."

* * *

A pale gazelle was already poking through the stone when Joseph put down the chisel. It was late. He would have to hurry to reach the house of worship before prayers began.

The twilight streets were crowded. Babylonia was so hot by day that people did their shopping and strolling in the evening. But Joseph ran quickly and didn't notice the crowds. He was still thinking about the little statue . . . the nostrils should flare out, the ears should be laid back, the tail . . . what should he do with the tail?

Oof! He crashed into a woman waiting at a street shrine. The chicken she was holding squawked loudly. "Watch out!" the woman yelled. "Stupid boy, you nearly ruined my offering to the gods."

"Sorry," he gasped and ran on.

The street was lined with shrines to many gods. People waited beside them with offerings of fruit, doves, and chickens. Joseph slowed down so as not to bump anybody else. "I'm not stupid, they're stupid," he thought scornfully. "How can they believe in so many gods when there's really only one God?"

The sky was already dark when he turned into the Jewish quarter. But across the river the sky glowed with orange flames from the torches atop the great temple of Marduk. Joseph shivered. Marduk was the cruel, powerful chief god of Babylonia. Everybody believed in him. As Zayyid had said, "We all belong to Marduk."

"Not me," he whispered and raced into the courtyard of the small synagogue.

Hayyim the caretaker was lighting the oil lamps in the whitewashed room when Joseph settled against the wall beside his father and grandfather. His father and uncles had helped to build this house of prayer before he was born. Nobody except grandfather remembered the Temple—the great one in Jerusalem that the Babylonians had destroyed. On hot summer nights when the family couldn't sleep, grandfather would retell how he and other Jews had been dragged from Judea to Babylonia as miserable captives.

"That's over," thought Joseph. "We're not miserable now." He turned to his father, eager to tell him, before prayer began, about the alabaster gazelle. But everybody was listening patiently as grandfather grumbled his usual complaints.

"You call this a house of God! This is a mud hut, a hovel! Solomon's Temple in Jerusalem—*that* was a house of God. Gold and ivory-covered walls, courtyards crowded with pilgrims from a hundred lands, air filled with the music of the Levites and thick with the smoke of sacrifices . . ."

Joseph's father interrupted, "Papa, Solomon's Temple is a heap of stones, and we Jews are captives here in Babylonia. We have no choice—we must accept our exile. And it's not so bad. We built a fine house of prayer. We study and pray. . . ."

"Feh," spat the old man, "this is no fine house of prayer. . . ."

Hayyim the caretaker interrupted before the argument could get hotter. He began to chant the opening blessing of the service, "Baruch Atah, Adonai Elohenu, Melech ha'olam. . . ." Joseph and the others quickly joined in, followed eventually by Grandfather who began to rock back and forth.

But the service ended almost before it began. Loud shouts from the street suddenly drowned out the singing.

"Long live King Cyrus!"

"Praise the great king!"

There was thunderous banging on the courtyard gate and shouts of "Open up. There's great news!"

Hayyim rushed out with the others close behind. "What happened? What's wrong?"

"King Cyrus has given us our freedom!" shouted a neighbor at the gate. "All the captive peoples of Babylonia can go home. The king proclaimed that we can take our treasures and return to our land to rebuild our Temple."

Grandpa pushed to the front. "Go back to Judea! Rebuild the Temple!" He raised his arms and danced about the courtyard. "Thank you God for letting me live to see this day. Long live King Cyrus!"

"Long live King Cyrus!" The cry echoed through the courtyard and through the whole Jewish quarter.

Festive bonfires blazed all through Babylonia that night. The city bustled with people from distant lands—Jews, Syrians, Phoenicians, and others who had been captured and dragged to Babylon as prisoners. In a dozen languages they praised the great Cyrus; they clapped, danced, and made plans to go home. Joseph, his brothers, parents, and grandfather danced with the others until long after midnight.

Later Joseph lay awake on the roof of his house, and he thought about Judea. "What will it be like? Will it be better than bustling Babylonia? What will I do there? Will I be able to carve beautiful things?" A tiny cloud of worry began to dampen his happiness.

*   *   *

In the next weeks Joseph's father and the heads of other families bought supplies, donkeys, and camels for the long trip. His mother packed dried dates and figs and prepared hard barley cakes.

But some Jews were expressing doubts.

"We have to cross the Syrian desert to reach Judea. It's a wilderness, full of snakes and scorpions. At night, evil spirits come out to eat travelers," whispered Joseph's friend, Abraham, as they sat and studied together.

In the house of prayer, Hayyim risked grandfather's wrath and argued, "Jerusalem is a graveyard. Jackals roam over the ruins. Why should I go back? Can't I be a good Jew here in Babylonia?"

"With my wife's stomach trouble I don't dare go," Isaac the potter explained.

Jacob the silversmith nodded. "I would love to help rebuild the Temple," he said, "but you know what a bad back I have."

Joseph's father stuck his chin out more stubbornly each day as the group of returning Jews grew smaller. "Better a small, strong group than a large, weak one," he said. But Joseph knew he was disturbed.

As the time to leave came closer, Zayyid the gem carver grew disturbed too. He had received an order from the palace for ten seals of carved jasper and five ivory antelopes. "Playful ones," the official said, "like the little leaping gazelle you showed me. And here's part payment for your work." The palace official dropped a gleaming gold coin into Zayyid's ready hand.

Zayyid drew in his breath. This was a gold stater, one of the valuable new coins from Lydia stamped with the clear pattern of a bull and a snarling lion. "Thank you, master," he said, bowing low.

After the official had gone, Zayyid chewed anxiously on the tip of his black beard. He could earn many such coins by working for the palace. But the palace wanted "playful antelopes," and, of all his workers, only Joseph could carve such antelopes.

"Joseph must remain in Babylonia," he muttered.

He stopped beside the boy one day and said, "What will a fine carver like you do in Judea?—dig ditches?"

"I'll make decorations for the Temple," Joseph answered uneasily.

"First you'll have to break your back, like a common slave, building the Temple walls," Zayyid sneered. "That's not proper work for you. Why should you go?"

"Because it's my homeland," said Joseph.

"Not all your people are going back. Why not stay here and work? Marduk will surely reward you and make you rich."

"I won't work for Marduk!" Joseph flared.

"No, of course not," Zayyid said soothingly. "Then Cyrus will reward you."

"My parents would not agree."

"I'll send a message to your parents," Zayyid said, "a very persuasive message." His eyes gleamed greedily under his thick eyebrows.

* * *

That evening Joseph carried home Zayyid's message, inscribed on a clay tablet, and a small, heavy leather pouch. "I know what I'll do," he thought happily. "If Mama and Papa agree, I'll stay here and carve for the king and get rich. And, as soon as the Temple is built, I'll go to Jerusalem and carve decorations. Everybody will be happy that way—me and Zayyid and my parents." He turned into his own street. There donkeys and camels stood tethered, and bundles lay ready to be loaded for the trip. Suddenly he thought, "But what if they don't agree?" He gritted his teeth. "Then I'll run away. I won't go to Judea to be a slave!"

His father's brows drew together as he read Zayyid's message. He opened the pouch and let the golden Lydian stater clatter onto the table. "A fat gold coin," he said in a hard, angry voice. "Zayyid values you highly."

He gripped Joseph's shoulders tightly and looked deep into his eyes. "Was it Zayyid's idea or yours to suggest that you remain in Babylonia?" he asked.

Joseph looked back defiantly. "It was Zayyid's idea, but I agree with him. I want to stay here and carve gems. I'll get rich, and then I'll come to Jerusalem and make beautiful things for the Temple."

Joseph's father took a deep breath and said slowly, "After fifty years of captivity, God has blessed us and allowed us to go home. Jerusalem is waiting for her children, for you and me, to come and rebuild her walls." He stuffed the coin back into the pouch. "Bring this bribe money back to Zayyid and say goodbye to him. The caravan to Judea is leaving before dawn tomorrow. I expect you to ride in it."

Joseph turned without a word and ran out the courtyard gate, past the bundles and camels and sheep, and on into the dark square. "I won't be a slave and dig ditches. I won't. I'm a carver," he gulped. His eyes were too blurry with tears to see two figures step out of the shadows. Suddenly a heavy blow knocked him to the ground. Something thick and scratchy was pulled over his head. The pouch was torn from his fingers, and his wrists were lashed together.

"The gold coin is still here. So the father refused my offer," growled a familiar voice. "Good. Now he'll have neither the gold nor the boy. They'll both belong to Marduk and me. Throw him into the cart."

Joseph listened groggily as Zayyid's voice rumbled above the rattle of the cart wheels. "We'll hide him in a temple storeroom until the caravan for Judea leaves. Once they're gone, he won't make any trouble. Turn left here toward the temple of Marduk."

Joseph's body rocked limply with the bouncing of the cart. But, as his head began to clear, Zayyid's terrifying words struck him—"They'll both belong to Marduk!"

Joseph stiffened angrily. "Zayyid tricked me," he thought. "He said I'd work like a slave to build the walls of Jerusalem. But, if I stay here in Babylonia, I'll be the slave of Zayyid and Marduk."

He twisted his body inside the sack. "I won't, I won't," he cried silently. His strong fingers strained at the cord that held his wrists. Slowly he felt it loosen.

The cart tipped upward, and the wheels rolled more smoothly. They were on the bridge crossing the river. The temple of Marduk was just ahead. With one desperate wrench, Joseph freed his wrists.

A moment later Zayyid turned to look. "Quiet as a lamb tied for the sacrifice," he laughed and turned back.

Joseph squirmed out of the heavy covering. He felt the edge of the cart, slid over it, and fell hard to the ground. Over and over he rolled sideways, scrambled to an archer's notch in the rail, and leaped through it into the black water.

Kicking off his sandals, Joseph swam toward shore, fighting the current that pulled him downstream. If Zayyid hadn't heard the splash, if he could make it to shore, if he could reach the Jewish quarter before dawn—if-if-if . . . "God of Abraham, please help me," he gasped.

*   *   *

The Jewish quarter sparkled with torches in the predawn darkness. Men prodded the groaning, complaining camels to their feet. Basket carriers on the donkey's sides were loaded with food and children. And neighbors crowded around the travelers to Judea, shouting blessings and goodbyes.

"Finish loading," called the caravan leader. "It's almost sunrise."

Joseph's mother seized her husband's arm. "How can we leave without Joseph?" she asked desperately.

He fussed with the camel harness to hide his tear-filled eyes. "Joseph is old enough to choose," he said gruffly. "By staying with Zayyid, he chose Babylonia over Judea." But he turned again and looked hopefully toward the dark square.

A bedraggled, limping figure was moving slowly into the torchlight.

"Joseph!" he cried. He ran to the boy, swept him up, and held him tight. Joseph's mother followed, sobbing, "Thank you, God, for bringing back our son."

"Mount up for Judea!" came the final call.

Many hands carried Joseph back to the caravan and set him on the camel behind his grandfather. With baaing and braying from the sheep and donkeys, and last hugs and kisses from those staying behind, the caravan formed into line. A woman's sweet, strong voice rose high above the clatter, singing, "Come, let us go up to the mountain of our God. Hallelujah, hallelujah. . . ."

"Hallelujah, hallelujah!" Joseph and his grandfather sang too, loudly enough to wake King Cyrus himself.

When the sky brightened to pink and gold, the caravan was already moving out of the city. Joseph turned for a last, shivery look at the looming temple of Marduk. Then he faced forward toward Jerusalem.

CHAPTER
4

"Who would want Number Four? It's smaller than a dime, and it's the color of mud and boring, with no pictures or anything," Jamie said.

"So what! Is this a beauty contest for coins?" Grandma asked tartly.

"I see a design." Sarah held the magnifying glass close. "It's like a stick figure. There's a design on back too. This time I'll look it up, and you can draw."

Only a few pages past the gold stater she found the picture and description of the small, dark coin.

BRONZE COIN, 2.3 grams weight, c. 167 B.C.E. Minted in Jerusalem for King Antiochus of Syria. A lily of Jerusalem appears on one side; on the other side, an anchor appears with an inscription in Greek, "Of King Antiochus the Benefactor."

Grandma leafed quickly through the history book. "I knew 167 B.C.E. was important!" she said triumphantly. "It was during the time that Antiochus, the Syrian king, ruled Judea. He forced the Jews to worship him and bow down to the Greek gods instead of following the laws of the Torah. The very next year the Maccabees started the revolt that drove the army of Antiochus out of Judea. It was the first war for religious freedom in the history of the world."

The Cave

Judea, c. 167 B.C.E.

The friskiest kid in the herd found the cave. It bounded up the mountainside chasing a butterfly and disappeared. A few minutes later Meir and Hayyim heard it bleating for help.

"That one gets into more trouble than my baby brother," Hayyim sighed and started up after it. Higher and higher he climbed until he reached a narrow ledge. The bleating sounded closer, muffled as though it were coming out of the ground.

"Where are you, you good-for-nothing?" Hayyim shouted. He inched along until, suddenly, with a startled "aiiiieeey!" he plunged down through a screen of scrub oak into a hole in the ledge.

"Meh-eh-ehhhhh" . . . screamed the little goat. Hayyim had landed on top of it.

"Help, Meir, help!" cried Hayyim.

Within minutes Meir reached the ledge. Both boys, lean, fair-haired Meir and stocky, dark Hayyim, pushed and pulled to drag the kicking kid up through the opening. It struggled to its feet with an indignant bleat and scrambled back down the mountainside.

"Grab my hand, and I'll pull you out," Meir called down. But Hayyim had disappeared from sight. A minute later his voice came echoing out of the hole, "There's a cave down here. It goes all the way back into the mountain."

"Are you sure? I never heard of a cave in this hill."

"Sure I'm sure. It's bigger than my whole house." Hayyim's voice squeaked with excitement as his cobwebby head appeared in the opening. "Help me up, then you can come down and look around."

"No. We have to get back to the herd." Meir braced himself and hoisted Hayyim out. "Let's come back later with an oil lamp and explore, and, if . . ."

". . . and, if it looks good, we'll make it our hideout," Hayyim continued. They were such good friends that they could easily finish each other's thoughts. "We'll bring up water and olives and figs. . . ."

". . . And it'll be a secret. We won't tell anyone else about it," Meir added.

"Right!"

For the next few Shabbat afternoons, and whenever they could sneak off in the evenings, the boys explored the cave. They came by roundabout paths and goat trails across the hills so that nobody would guess where they were going. Long-legged Meir bounded ahead lightly, and stubby Hayyim puffed along behind. But, when they reached the hideout, Hayyim became the leader. He would lean back and stare at the rocky ceiling, and an idea would pop into his head. "Let's braid a ladder out of vines or make a springy mattress of branches or build a tiny table for supplies," he'd say. And they would get to work.

They brought along olives, figs, raisins, and water. Through a narrow opening in the cliff face, they had a view of the valley and of their village on the opposite hill.

One day Hayyim sat at the opening thinking. "Meir," he said, "this is as good as the lookout tower of a fortress. We can see the village, but the villagers can't see us."

"Yeah, look down by the path," Meir whispered. "Is that your cousin Eli walking into the olive grove with Rachel the potter's daughter?"

"Uh-huh," Hayyim said absently. "Meir," he said suddenly, "this cave would make a terrific fortress. We could fight the whole Greek army from here."

Meir turned reluctantly away from Eli and Rachel. "Why would we want to fight the Greek army?" he asked.

"Because they're our enemies."

"They are not. My father says they're the best rulers Judea could have. He says that if it weren't for stubborn, old men like Mattathias in Modin we'd get along with them perfectly."

"*My* father says we'll have to fight them sooner or later. So let's pretend that this is our fortress and we have to get it ready for battle. All right?"

"Well, all right. As long as we're just pretending," Meir said doubtfully.

Hayyim started planning. "First we have to make weapons. I know how to make a bow and arrows. I'll ask Hanan the sandal maker how to make strong string."

"Spears are easy." Meir was getting interested. "We can get branches from the olive trees in the valley. Let's go down now. Maybe we'll surprise Eli and Rachel."

They slipped from boulder to boulder, down the hill and into the grove. Eli and Rachel were nowhere to be seen, but the boys found piles of branches newly pruned from the trees. They brought the straightest ones back up to the ledge and began to trim them while they made plans for their fortress.

But, before a week had gone by, before the boys could whittle a single arrow, Hayyim's and Meir's parents made decisions that ruined the boys' plans.

First, Hayyim's father announced that Hayyim was finished with herding goats and would now begin full-time study at the village school. After school he would work at the family's grain mill.

Second, Meir's father, the town's richest merchant, was chosen by the Greek authorities to be the town tax collector. To suit his high position, he shaved off his beard, ordered three stylish Greek tunics—short enough to show off his knobby knees—and hired a Greek tutor to educate Meir.

Many days passed before Hayyim and Meir were able to return to the cave. This time they had to circle and crouch low to hide from a squad of Greek soldiers camped in the valley.

"I hate them!" Hayyim growled as he stared through the lookout. "I wish we had our bows and arrows so we could shoot up their whole camp."

"They're not so bad," Meir said. "I like my teacher, and I'm learning some funny stories about the Greek gods."

"Very funny!" said Hayyim angrily. "The Greeks want us to bring gifts to their silly gods; they want us to eat pigs and stop keeping Shabbat."

"That's just talk," Meir said. "They'll get over it. You have to see their good side, Hayyim. The Greeks have great gymnasiums where they wrestle and do other sports. My teacher is going to take me to a gym. He says I might be a good runner. Why don't you come too?"

Hayyim spat an olive pit through the lookout opening with such force that it flew halfway down the hill. "I have to go home," he snapped and scrambled up the ladder.

Hayyim and Meir had never disagreed about anything before. They both felt terrible, but they didn't know how to settle their differences—so they stayed away from each other. It was difficult. All their lives they had played and studied and herded goats together. They missed each other. Finally one evening Meir waited for Hayyim at the doorway of the mill.

"Are you mad at me?" he asked.

"No . . . but . . ."

"Then let's meet at the hideout again."

Hayyim took a deep breath. "All right," he said, "tomorrow, after sundown."

"Oh. Tomorrow I have to . . ." Meir began.

"What?"

"Nothing. Forget it. But, if I'm late, wait for me."

* * *

Hayyim came early the next day and watched through the lookout as shadows filled the trees and fields of the valley. The darkness crept up the hillside toward the village, catching the donkeys and farmers who were slowly coming home. Meir was late. Maybe he wasn't coming. Hayyim was ready to leave when he saw a flash of blue under the olive trees. A short while later pebbles rattled down the opening, and Meir leaped into the cave.

"Hayyim, Hayyim—I was in a race today, and I won!" In the lamplight his body shone with sweat and oil, and his face glowed with excitement. "You won't believe it! I can't believe it either. I'm the best twelve-year-old runner in all of Judea! You should've seen me. I was way out in front the whole time."

Meir was wearing only a blue cloak. The high-laced sandals of a Greek athlete covered his long legs up to the knee. Hayyim thought suddenly, "He looks as handsome as one of the statues the Greeks put in the market-place." Hayyim felt small and clumsy—and jealous. "You look like a stork," he blurted. "Go home and get dressed."

But Meir didn't hear. He was too full of his own news. "Jason, my teacher, says I'm a natural athlete, and, if I train and build up my wind and my legs, I might run in the Olympics someday. Isn't that great?"

Hayyim drew back from his friend. "But you're a Jew. Why do you want to run in games that honor the Greek gods?" he asked in amazement.

"Because, because . . ." Meir searched for words, "because it's fun to run and because Jason says it's a gift to the gods to make your body as beautiful and perfect as you can."

"That's a stupid gift for stupid gods!" Hayyim burst out. "Our God doesn't want us to look beautiful and run around like rabbits. Our God wants us to study Torah and follow the laws and be good to each other."

"Don't get mad again," Meir pleaded. He sat down beside Hayyim and put a hand on his shoulder. "You don't understand about the gods and about sports because you're ignorant. You know only the old customs that you learn in school—like not letting slaves work on the Sabbath or circumcising baby boys. Those customs are uncivilized."

"They're God's commandments!" Hayyim shouted. He shook off Meir's hand. "My sister's new baby will be circumcised tomorrow. Are you saying that's uncivilized?"

"Yes!" Meir shouted back. "And not only that, it's against the law."

"Against whose law? Greek law? Any Jew who believes in Greek law is a traitor. And that means you're a traitor. I'm not your friend any more!"

Hayyim climbed out of the cave and stumbled down the hill, barely seeing his way through a blur of furious tears.

*   *   *

There was angry talk in the village about the new decrees of the Greek rulers. No circumcision, no Torah study, no Sabbath. People argued in the mill and in the town square. Some said, "Just go along with the laws for a short time. They'll forget." Others said, "We'll never give in. We'll die first." Hayyim's little nephew was circumcised quietly. And Hayyim studied and worked and missed his friend—hated him but missed him.

One day as he squatted in the mill, filling baskets with grain, Hayyim felt a hand on his shoulder. "I need half a drachma's worth of flour," said a familiar voice.

Hayyim stood up, avoiding Meir's eyes. He took the bronze coin and went to the flour bin.

Meir followed. "I have to talk to you. It's important," he said.

"Nothing you have to say to me is important."

"Listen to me. Don't be a stubborn, stiff-necked peasant," Meir whispered.

Hayyim turned angrily and pushed him with all his might. Meir fell, dragging the smaller boy with him. They rolled on the flour-covered earth, punching, wrestling, and trying to pin each other down. Flour swirled up and covered them as they thrashed and struggled.

"Traitor, idol worshiper, I hate you!" Hayyim sobbed as he fought. But Meir fought silently and finally ended up on top, straddling Hayyim's chest and pinning down his arms.

"Give up!" he gasped.

"Never!"

"Then listen." He leaned close to the squirming, kicking boy and panted in a harsh whisper, "Your family is in danger."

Hayyim stopped kicking.

"The Greek captain told my father that there will be a search tonight

for circumcised babies. The Greeks will kill them and their mothers. Get your sister and her baby out of the village."

"There's no time. Where can they go?" Hayyim asked wildly.

A bellowing voice silenced them as Hayyim's father came running from the yard. "Shame on you! Are you pagans? Fighting like village dogs! Get up!"

Meir jumped up and pulled Hayyim up. They were white with flour except for their frightened, staring eyes. Soundlessly Meir formed the words, "Take them to the hideout."

* * *

At twilight Hayyim led three young families over the hills on the twisting path that led to the cave. They carried water, food, and three infant boys. Through the long night they waited. When the moon was at its highest, painting the olive trees silvery-gray, they heard a faint bugle call, then sharp commands and cries from the village. At dawn they watched as a squad of Greek soldiers spread out to search the hills. Footsteps rasped on the rocks below the ledge, but the oak shrubs were a sturdy screen. The footsteps moved on.

In the middle of the second night, Hayyim was jolted awake by the sound of pebbles dropping into the cave. He gripped his club tightly, raised it . . . and dropped it when he heard, "It's me, Meir."

Two dark shapes slid down through the opening. Meir's fair hair gleamed even in the darkness. He pushed the other man forward. "This is Enoch. Your father sent him," he said softly. "He fights with Mattathias and his sons."

Enoch spoke in a gruff, urgent voice. "The search is over for now, but you can't go back. They'll be watching for you. Wake the others. I'll lead you to safety higher in the mountains."

Meir turned to climb out of the cave.

"Wait!" Hayyim grabbed his arm. "Aren't you coming with us?"

He shook his head silently.

"But you're a Jew, and you're my best friend. Don't stay with the Greeks, please. You belong with me," he pleaded.

Meir's eyes were dark hollows in the shadowy blur of his face. He looked down at his high-laced sandals and then at Hayyim. "I don't know where I belong," he said. Gently he put off Hayyim's hand and swung up the ladder. At the top he leaned down and whispered, "God be with you. Maybe someday we'll meet here in the cave again."

CHAPTER
5

The dark, rough surface of coin Number Five seemed to soak up the low, slanted rays of sunlight.

"It's like a black hole in the table," said Jamie.

"This one gives me the shivers. I wonder if it had a sad life," said Sarah.

"Let's find out." Grandma held the coin at arm's length and squinted. "I see a tree on one side and writing on the other. And there's a hole right above the tree. Maybe somebody wore it on a chain.

Sarah drew the coin in the notebook while Jamie hunted through the first three chapters of the book of coins until he found it.

BRONZE HALF-SHEKEL, 69
Minted in Jerusalem by Jews rebelling against Roman rule. On one side appear a palm tree with two baskets of dates and the Hebrew inscription, "For the redemption of Zion." On the other side appear two lulavim and an etrog and the Hebrew inscription, "Year Four."

"You were right, Sarah. It is a sad coin," Grandma said. "It was made during the fourth year of the war that the Jews fought against the mighty Roman Empire."

"First they fought Antiochus, and then they took on the whole Roman Empire," Jamie exclaimed. "Wow, they were gutsy people!"

Grandma shook her head. "Gutsy, but not realistic. It was a hopeless fight. By the end of the war the Temple was burned to the ground and the survivors were carried off as slaves. For the next 1,900 years the Jews had no land of their own. This coin marked the beginning of the Jewish exile from the Land of Israel."

A Fair Trade

Rome, 70

"Victory parades are supposed to be fun," thought seven-year-old Esther, "but this one is going to be terrible."

First, her mother wouldn't buy her a sugar bun or a tiny Roman eagle on a stick. Second, her father said that this was a very sad parade for the Jews because it meant that the Romans had crushed the Jewish rebellion in Judea. So she must not shout or cheer. "What's a rebellion?" Esther wondered. "And what fun is a parade if you can't cheer?" Third, the main avenue in Rome was so crowded that she and her friend Claudia couldn't see anything.

When she asked, "Papa, please pick me up," her father didn't answer. Her parents were standing close together, as if they were holding each other up, and their faces were tight and sad in the middle of the excited, laughing crowd.

Esther and Claudia bent way down and wiggled their way, headfirst, between the arms and legs of the grownups until they reached the edge of the avenue. High above, the golden eagle of the Roman legion swept past on a pole. Rows and rows of huge, sunburned soldiers marched behind it with armor jingling and spears and swords held ready.

The crowd began to shout, "Long live the legion! Long live the emperor!" Claudia shouted too, but Esther just moved her lips and waved at the marching men. As the pounding of their steps died out, she heard a dragging, shuffling sound. Lines of panting, perspiring slaves were moving up the avenue, pulling wagons loaded with sparkling gold and silver.

"Yech, they smell bad," Claudia whispered and held her nose.

Esther didn't notice. She was staring at the first wagon, where a huge, golden menorah stood, as tall as a man. "Th-that's our menorah," she

stammered. "It's the Jewish menorah from the Temple in Jerusalem. My father told me about it. Why is it here?"

"Huh?" Claudia stared at her.

The crowd began to shout, "Jerusalem is lost! Long live the legion!" Claudia turned to watch, but Esther looked wildly for her parents. They would tell her what was happening. Waiting for the next group of marchers, people pressed so closely around her that she couldn't move.

More bugle calls sounded, more soldiers and eagles and pennants passed.

And then, behind them, stumbled endless gray lines of men, women, and children, chained together, with heads lowered and eyes staring at the stone pavement.

"They're Jews," Esther realized with horror. "They're my family." She searched the gray lines for the Judean uncle and aunt she had once met. But all the prisoners looked alike. Now the crowd was chanting, "Jerusalem is ours . . . Judea is Roman." Esther felt a choking lump in her throat. She turned and, with all her strength, pushed back through the swaying, cheering people.

"Come back," Claudia yelled. "You'll miss the best part."

But Esther's father had already caught her hand, and the family hurried home.

From inside their house, near the marketplace of Rome, they could hear the rising roar of the crowd as the Judean prisoners reached the throne of the emperor. It became a joyous, whooping scream when the Jewish leaders of the revolt against Rome were strangled before the eyes of the royal party.

Esther's father covered his ears and sank onto a bench. "Our people are prisoners; the Temple is destroyed," he moaned. "How will God hear us now that the Gates of Prayer are closed?"

Esther began to cry too. "If the Temple is gone, where will God live? Will God leave us?"

Her mother pulled her into her lap. "God can't abandon us. We're the chosen people," she said. "God will be with us wherever we go—even here in Rome." Then she wiped her eyes and began to take off her bracelets. "We want to mourn for the Temple," she said, "but first it's more important to redeem the captives. We'll collect all the gold and silver we have, even your little gold earrings. The elders of the synagogue will need the wealth of all the Jews of Rome to buy freedom for the prisoners."

That day they carried their small bag of treasure through the festive streets to the synagogue. Then they closed the doors and shutters. Esther's parents put ashes on their heads and, for a week, they sat on the floor, crying for the lost Temple, for the ruined city of Jerusalem, and for their fellow Jews who had been killed or enslaved.

It was the longest, saddest week of Esther's life. But, finally, one morning when she awoke, she heard grain being pounded in the courtyard and kittens mewing beside the milk pail. The sound of hammering came from her father's carpentry shop. "We're done!" she yelled and pulled on her linen shirt, twisted her hair into a braid, and ran to the shop.

"Papa," she cried, "are we finished being sad?"

Her father laid down his mallet and lifted her in a hug. "Little Esther, we'll be sad until that day when you and I and Mama can go up to the rebuilt city of Jerusalem and bring gifts to God in the Temple," he said. "Until then, even though we're sad, we'll keep on living and carrying out God's laws."

"Can we be a little bit happy while we're sad?" Esther asked hopefully. "Like, can I go out and play with Claudia?"

"Go," he said, "but first I have something to give you." He took a bronze coin, threaded on a leather thong, from a hook on the wall. "This is a half-shekel from Judea. Our brothers and sisters made it while they were fighting the Romans. See the writing on it? 'For the Redemption of Zion.' " He slipped the thong over her head. "Now, even when you're playing, this coin will remind you of Jerusalem."

Esther ran her fingers over the coin. "I'll try to remember," she said.

From the courtyard her mother called, "You have only a little while to play. Tonight is Shabbat. I'll need your help."

"Shabbat, hurray!" Esther stuffed some flat barley bread rubbed with garlic into her sash, grabbed her doll, and raced out to the street.

"Claudia, come out and bring your doll," Esther shouted over the neighboring brick wall.

Claudia's smooth, brown hair, held in a bright headband, popped up from the other side. "I'm coming," she said, "and wait till you see what I have. It's better than a doll."

"Move before I beat you, stupid thing!" Esther heard Claudia scolding. Then Claudia appeared at the gate, puffed up like a proud rooster. She was tugging along a tiny, thin girl, no more than four years old, wearing a ragged shirt.

"Who's this? Your cousin?" Esther asked.

"Of course not," Claudia said huffily. "Do you think I'd have such a skinny, grubby-looking cousin? She's my slave! My mother gave her to me. My mother said she's worthless because she's too little. My father got her for nothing when he bought three big Nubians for his warehouse."

Esther bent to peek at the small girl's face. Two large, frightened eyes peeked back at her from under a tangle of black hair. "What's her name?" she asked.

"I call her 'Dummy' because she won't talk."

"But what's her real name?"

Claudia shrugged. "I don't know."

Esther tapped the girl's thin shoulder. She shivered and pulled back. "She feels like a bird who flew into our house once, all bony and trembly, poor thing. Girl, what's your name?"

The little one didn't raise her head.

"See?" said Claudia. "She's a dummy."

"Is it Clovis . . . Helen . . . Juno?" Esther asked. There was no answer. "Or maybe Yohevet . . . Leah . . . Rivkah?" Esther added, trying some Hebrew names.

The large, dark eyes trembled upward, but they dropped again as Claudia broke in impatiently. "Come on, Esther, let's play. Forget about Dummy. She's no fun."

Claudia looped the little slave's harness over the gatepost. "Let's play shopkeeper and lady. You can be the lady because you have a new necklace."

"It's not a necklace!" Esther's hand flew up to cover the half-shekel. Then she turned away and picked up her doll. She felt the eyes of the sad, little girl following her.

Claudia squatted behind a broken grindstone. "What can I sell you today, my lady?" she whined.

"I need three hundred of your juiciest, pickled peacock tongues," Esther ordered, "and a basketful of honeyed figs and a jug of sweet, red wine."

Claudia scurried along the roadside collecting the "food." "Here you are, my lady," she said at last, placing pebbles, twigs, and a nutshell filled with water on the stone. "Now you have to pay me two hundred drachmas."

"Oh, where is my money?" Esther pretended to search for her purse. "I must have left it at home."

"Don't worry, my lady. You can pay me with that funny coin you're wearing on your neck."

"No, I can't." Esther tucked the coin under her shirt. "My father gave it to me. It's not a toy."

"He won't care. It's not real money." Claudia's eyes sparkled with interest. She hated to be refused anything.

"I'll pay with something better," Esther said quickly. She pulled out the bread and garlic and broke it into three parts. "Here's a piece for you," she said as she handed one part to Claudia, "and a piece for me, and a piece for Dummy."

She reached past Claudia to where the tiny slave crouched by the gate. "Come on, little one," she said. "Take a piece. You'll like it."

"Don't bother," said Claudia. "She doesn't eat anything—except sometimes a carrot or a turnip. My mother gave her a piece of meat last night, but she jumped away as if it were poison. She gets skinnier each day. Mama says not to worry about it because she didn't cost anything."

"That's strange," said Esther as she chewed her bread.

"Not so strange. You won't eat in my house either," Claudia pouted.

An idea struck Esther so suddenly that she gulped and started choking on her bread. When Claudia pounded her on the back, Esther coughed and gasped. Meanwhile her thoughts raced, "Claudia's food isn't kosher. That's why I can't eat at her house. Does Dummy eat only kosher? Could she be Jewish? One of the Jewish prisoners?"

Esther's mother called from the yard, "Esther, come in now. I need your help to get ready for Shabbat."

At the word "Shabbat" the little girl raised glowing, questioning eyes. Her lips trembled.

"Her eyes are telling me," Esther thought excitedly. "She's a Judean!"

Trying to keep her voice from shaking, Esther turned to Claudia and said, "Dummy is no fun at all, is she? Let's trade. I'll give you my big doll, the one my father made out of cedar wood."

"Why do you want her if she's no fun?" Claudia asked suspiciously.

"What shall I tell her?" Esther thought desperately. "If I tell the truth, she'll never let me have the little girl. She loves to tease."

"Uh . . . uh . . . I'll get her to do my chores," Esther said hurriedly.

"Well . . . I don't mind," said Claudia, preparing to bargain. "But a real, live slave is worth a lot more than a doll."

"But that's all I have!" Esther tried to keep her voice cool.

Claudia's eyes narrowed shrewdly. "You can give me the doll and that funny coin, the one you're wearing around your neck."

"I can't!" Esther cried. "My father said . . ."

"Forget it." Claudia turned and yanked at the little girl's harness. "Come on," she ordered. The girl fell forward and then scrambled to her feet.

"Redeem the captives"—the words popped into Esther's head. "Mama said that was most important of all. . . . Wait!" she cried. "I'll give it to you." With shaking hands she lifted the thong with the bronze half-shekel over her head and gave it to Claudia. Then Esther bent and lifted the small girl who weighed no more than the cedar doll.

"Don't be scared," Esther said. "I'm taking you home."

CHAPTER

6

"Tch, tch, tch," Grandma clucked, looking up at her teapot-shaped clock. "The afternoon is going too fast." She hurried to the stove to set up a split pea soup for supper.

"Yeah, really," Jamie said. "In one hour we covered more than 2,000 years."

"From Jericho to Rome," Sarah added. She turned to the next small coin. "Where will you take us, Number Six?"

Jamie held the magnifying glass close. "On one side there's a man's head with a crown or a ring on it," he said, "and on the other there are two funny shapes . . . no, two horses with men riding them. And there's writing around the edge."

Grandma put a bowl of grapes on the table. Sarah munched while she turned pages. Finally, she called out, "Here it is!"

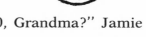

BRONZE DENARI, c. 190
Minted in Rome. On one side appears the profile of Geta, the Roman Caesar. On the other side appear two horsemen and an inscription in Latin.

"Did anything special happen around the year 190, Grandma?" Jamie asked.

"There were no wars, thank goodness," Grandma said. "But the Romans were rulers of the Land of Israel. They called it Palestine. While some

Jews still lived in Palestine, others were scattered all over the world. The rabbis were busily writing down Jewish laws so that they wouldn't be forgotten by Jews in those other lands. These writings were called the Mishnah. They became part of the Talmud, and we still study them today."

The Rememberer

Galilee, c.190

Savta Nehama was the oldest person in the family, and Rivka was the youngest. They both loved to walk and pick flowers and talk. But Savta usually had more to say because she had learned more in her seventy years than Rivka had learned in her eight years. She told stories about witches, animals, kings, and queens, each with a special meaning. And Rivka loved to figure out the meanings. One day Savta told a story that made Rivka feel a little better about getting kicked!

* * *

Rivka was on her way back from the town well, carrying a clay basin of water in her hands and a bunch of pink wildflowers for her grandmother under her arm. She passed a sad, hot, drooping horse standing beside the bakery. He wore a jingling Roman harness, which meant that he belonged to a soldier. Because Rivka felt sorry for him, she stopped to give him a drink. Suddenly a voice roared, "Take your hands off my horse!" Before she could jump away, Rivka was flung into the air by a hard kick in the rear. The water splashed out and the flowers scattered. Rivka scrambled to her feet, clutching the basin, and raced for home.

Savta was sitting in the courtyard shaping bread dough into small patties. She listened as Rivka told her what had happened. "I hate the Romans! Why are they so mean?" Rivka exclaimed when she finished the story.

"Sit," said Savta. "Help me shape the bread. My hands ache."

"But, Savta, you're not answering me!"

"Sit," the lean, little woman commanded. As Rivka plopped down with her lower lip trembling, ready to cry, her grandmother tipped her head to one side and said, "Let me tell you the story of the stork and the lion.

"Once a lion got a bone stuck deep in its throat. It roared and yowled

and tried to get the bone out, but it wouldn't budge. A stork flapped down, watched the lion, and finally said, 'I have a long bill. I'll stick it down your throat and pull out the bone.'

" 'Oh, thank you,' cried the lion. 'I'll be so grateful that I'll pay you any price you ask.'

"The stork stuck its long bill and its head deep into the lion's mouth and pulled out the bone. Then the stork sat back and waited to be paid. Instead, the lion roared, 'Get out of here!'

" 'How about my pay?' the stork protested.

" 'You stuck your head into a lion's mouth and pulled it safely out again. That's payment enough,' the lion roared."

*   *   *

With a slap slap, the grandmother's wrinkled hands turned and flattened the dough on the smooth rock. Rivka's hands moved more slowly as she tried to understand. Her grandmother always explained things by telling stories. She was known in the village as a wise woman, one who remembered the teachings of the sages.

"You mean the lion is like the Romans, and we Jews are like the stork? And we can't expect them to be nice to us, even if we're nice and give their horses a drink? We just have to be grateful that they leave us alone?"

Savta nodded.

"Well that's awful! If they're so bad, I think we should throw them out. This is our village, not their's."

Her grandmother's hands rested wearily on the dough. Her eyes looked far past Rivka's flushed, angry face, up to the hills around the village. "We tried many times," she said. "Oh, how we tried. And finally we learned that we can never beat the Romans by using swords and chariots."

"What then?"

"We have to fight by following God's words and living as Jews. That's why your father and the other rabbis are writing down the words of the sages and the laws of our people."

Rivka made a face. Talking about laws didn't make her feel better. All she wanted at that moment was to kick a Roman soldier.

Savta understood. Her eyes twinkled from deep in their web of wrinkles, and she tipped her head again. "Did I ever tell you the story that Rabbi Akiva told my grandfather about the fox and the fishes?" she asked. Without waiting for an answer, she handed Rivka another blob of dough and began, "A hungry fox came to the shore of the sea on a wild, stormy day. . . ." But she stopped telling the story as she noticed that Rivka's father was waiting respectfully at the gate, holding a clay tablet.

"Yes, my son?"

"Reb Pinchas, Reb Naftali, and I are writing about the holidays, and we are confused about the day on which the new year of the trees is to be observed."

Savta closed her eyes and sat silently for a few seconds. Then she began to rock back and forth as she related, "The school of Rabbi Hillel taught that the new year of the trees is to be observed on the fifteenth day of Shevat. This is what my great-grandfather told my grandfather, and my grandfather told me. But the school of Rabbi Shammai taught that the new year comes on the first of Shevat. Rabbi Hillel was concerned for the poor people whose trees, growing in poor soil, would bear fruit later. Shammai sided with the rich people."

Rivka's father wrote a quick note. Then he looked up and said, "Our rabbis make a fence around the Torah by adding explanations and new laws. But it's an endless job to write down the laws before they are forgotten. Thank God that you remember so much, Mama. May you live until a hundred and twenty."

Savta shook her head. "Not until a hundred and twenty." Then she reached over and playfully mussed Rivka's hair. "But this little one remembers every word I tell her. Teach her to read and write, and she'll be a great help to you."

"But, she's a girl!" Rivka's father said uneasily.

"Beruriah, the wife of Rabbi Meir, was once a girl, and she became a great scholar. I was once a girl too!" Savta snapped.

After that day Rivka's father took time from his work as a carver in the tombs on the hillsides of Bet Shearim and taught Rivka to read and write.

* * *

When the autumn rains began, the dry, brown hills suddenly sparkled with wildflowers. Savta insisted on walking in the drizzle. She leaned on her stick with one hand, on Rivka's shoulder with the other, and breathed the flower smells hungrily. "As though this is her last chance," Rivka thought sadly. She reached up and put her warm hand over her grandmother's cold one.

One day, as they walked, a caravan of horses, brightly dressed riders, and camels carrying litters came toward them. "They're bringing the body of a rich Jew from Babylonia to be buried here in our village," said Rivka's grandmother. "Your father will have a lot of work to carve a fine tomb for him."

"All the way from Babylonia? Why?" Rivka asked.

"He wanted to be buried near the graves of the great teachers and sages, here in Bet Shearim, so that on Judgment Day he might share the honor that is due them." She laughed and added, "As for me—I don't want a tomb. Just bury me with my walking stick. On the day of deliverance I want to jump up to greet the Messiah."

Rivka giggled to think of her tiny, bent grandmother jumping and waving her stick at the Messiah. Savta laughed too and showered Rivka with petals.

The winds grew stronger. Rain pounded the earthen roof and trickled down the stone walls of the house. The family moved up to the raised part of the floor and brought the goats and sheep into the lower part to help keep the room warm. Rivka's father took the last few denari from

the clay jug hidden in the eaves to buy charcoal for the fire. But Savta's legs and arms grew stiff and achey. Rivka spent long hours reading to her and listening to the stories and teachings of the wise men. Each story began, "I heard this from my grandfather, who heard it from his father, who heard it from Rabbi Hillel"—or Shammai, or Meir, or one of the other rabbis of long ago. Again Rivka had the sad feeling that her grandmother was racing against time, trying to tell as much as she could.

One night the house shook with blasts of wind, and Savta shivered and said, "I'm ready to die, but I want to see the first flowers once more. I want to see the almond tree covered with white blossoms."

Rivka moved closer, trying to warm Savta's thin body. "Hold on, Savta," she whispered.

Savta Nehama died the week before the new year of the trees. Her body and her stout walking stick were carried through the cold rain to the family's burial cave. When the seven days of mourning were over, the almond trees were wearing their white blossoms. But Rivka couldn't bear to look at them. "Why couldn't Savta wait? Or why couldn't the trees hurry?"

She missed the feeling of her grandmother's hand on her shoulder when she walked. She missed Savta's smile, and the way Savta tipped her head to the side before saying, "Did I tell you the story of. . . ."

"Stop moping," said Rivka's mother. "Go and play with Hannah, next door."

Rivka shook her head.

The fig trees began to leaf, and poppies sprang up from between the rocks. Passover came and went. On late afternoons and evenings the scholars left their fields and workshops and sat under the fig tree near Rivka's house to continue thinking through and writing down the teachings of the sages. When Rivka was in the courtyard pounding grain or picking pebbles out of the beans, she heard them talking. It made her sad again— and lonely.

One evening the quiet talk changed to loud shouts. Rivka's father's voice cried, "You're wrong! All the sages believed in the coming of the Messiah!" And Rabbi Naftali's voice rumbled in reply, "Rabbi Yochanan ben Zakkai gave it very little importance!"

"Oh, no," Rivka thought, "that's not what Savta said." Forgetting to be timid with the learned men, Rivka called out, "Savta said that her grandfather told her, that his grandfather told him, that Rabbi Yochanan said, 'If you are busy planting, and somebody tells you that the Messiah is coming, finish planting and then go and greet him.'"

There was no sound from the men under the fig tree. Only the crickets kept sawing away in the warm, night air. Then feet rustled in the dry grass. Rivka looked up to see four eager-eyed, bearded faces, each with a black tefillin box bound to his forehead. "You remember this?" her father asked her, speaking for the others.

Rivka was surprised at the question. "Of course," she said. "I remember everything Savta told me, and everything we read together."

"Ah," sighed her father, "we've lost one rememberer, may she rest in peace, and God has given us another to help us in our work."

"Praised be God. The chain continues unbroken," murmured the others.

Rivka let the beans fall through her fingers as a happy thought came to her. "If I'm part of the chain, and Savta is part of the chain, then it's as if we're still touching each other!"

She jumped up to bring the beans inside. "Mama," she called, "tomorrow I'll ask Hannah if she wants to pick flowers for Shavuot with me."

CHAPTER
7

Number Seven shone bright and golden in the light of the kitchen lamp.

"This one looks happy," Sarah laughed. "I'll bet it lived in a good time. It has such a pretty, wavy design."

"That pretty, wavy design is Arabic writing," said Grandma. "The next coin, Number Eight, has Arabic writing too."

"Arabic writing!" Jamie mumbled. His fingers flew through the pages of the coin book. "Yikes! There are a hundred coins with Arabic writing."

"Slow down and look carefully. You'll find them both," Grandma said.

Jamie slowed down, and there they were, right under his fingers—a gold dinar and a silver dirhem.

GOLD DINAR, c. 800
Coined in Baghdad, Babylonia. Like most Islamic coins, it follows the laws of the Koran which forbid the use of images. Instead of pictures of animals or people, this coin is inscribed with Arabic text. On one side there is the phrase, "Mohammed is the apostle of God." On the other side is the name of the caliph, "Al Mansur."

"You guessed right, Sarah," said Grandma. "The gold dinar comes from a very happy time in our history. Many Jews were living in Babylonia by 800—more than in Palestine. The rulers of the country were usually friendly and allowed the Jews to control their own affairs. A Jewish prince ruled the community, and there were great schools where scholars studied and argued over the laws of the Torah and the Talmud. The arguments sometimes became so fierce that they split the Jewish community.

Pepper Pot's Pidyon Haben

Babylonia, c.800

Penina's new nephew had a wrinkled, red face and fists as tiny as walnuts. And when he cried he mewed like a kitten.

"A voice like a rabbi," proclaimed Penina's mother, the proud new grandmother. "He'll be a teacher in the academy at Sura some day, God willing."

"Such an intelligent face," said Leah, the next-door neighbor, as the baby opened his mouth in a great, toothless yawn.

"And long fingers like a scribe. Just like his grandfather's, no evil eye should harm them," Leah's husband added.

"I think he's funny-looking," said eight-year-old Penina.

"Penina Pepper Pot, mind your sharp tongue," her mother scolded. But the baby's mother smiled and said, "He'll be fatter and prettier by the day of his pidyon haben."

In the next few weeks it seemed to Penina that everybody in Sura, Babylonia, was coming to see the new baby. She was kept busy all day carrying out grapes and stuffed dates and cool lemon water for the guests. Everybody came except her favorite uncle, red-bearded Amnon, and his wife Esther.

Amnon was the one who had given her the nickname "Pepper Pot" because she had hair as red as pepper—just like his—and because she always said exactly what she thought—even when it got her into trouble. Amnon used to swing her in circles and give her rides on his shoulders. Of course, now that she was old enough to wear earrings and pin up her curly braids, he didn't swing her anymore. But he was still her favorite.

"When is Uncle Amnon coming to see the new baby?" Penina asked several days later while she and her mother were stuffing dates with almonds and walnuts.

Her mother's beaming, round face grew sober, and her eyes filled with tears. "He won't be coming," she said.

"Why not?"

"Because he's angry with us. He has become a Karaite, a follower of the priest Anan. He says that we're not good Jews, and he can't come to our house anymore."

"But he has to come. I miss him," Penina exclaimed. "Besides, he's a kohen. We need him to redeem the baby at the pidyon haben."

"We'll get another kohen," her mother said abruptly. "And I don't want to hear another word about Amnon. You're too young to understand such matters!" She thrust a basket at Penina. "Go . . . go and pick some lemons."

Penina kicked pebbles all the way out to the lemon tree in the courtyard. "I do too understand," she fumed. "Mama is really sad because Amnon and Esther won't come. If they knew, they'd be sorry, and then they would surely come. Someone ought to tell them about the ceremony."

"Why, someone?" she thought, as she yanked off a lemon. "Why not *me?* I'll go and tell them right now." She dropped the lemon and skipped out to the dusty street. It was a short walk to the market and then a much longer walk down the twisting lanes past the workshops of the potters and the silversmiths. At last she reached the lane of the leather workers.

"Welcome, Pepper Pot," Amnon cried when he saw her blinking in the doorway of his shadowed shop. He put down the sandal he was cutting, wiped his hands, and pulled her to sit beside him at his workbench.

"You're getting so tall. And you've put up your braids. I would never know you if I passed you on the street."

Penina giggled. She was glad to see that Amnon's beard was as red and bushy as ever and that his eyes still crinkled merrily. But he had lost his round belly, and there were new, deep lines on his forehead. She wondered if it was because he was a Ka . . . Kara . . . or whatever her mother had called him.

"How is the new baby?" Amnon asked.

"That's just why I came," Penina said eagerly, "to ask you to please, please come to the pidyon haben. Mama is making roasted lamb and almonds, just the way you like it. And she'll be so happy if you're there."

Amnon stiffened and turned away. Then he answered in a harsh voice, "I would like to come, but I can't. Your family is disobeying God's law."

"We are not!" Penina said indignantly. "Papa is a scribe. He knows God's law. He wouldn't let us disobey it."

Amnon's face turned redder than his beard. "Your father is following the preachings of the rabbis instead of the Torah," he exclaimed and pounded his fist on the bench. "Oil lamps burn in your house on Shabbat even though the Torah forbids it." He banged again. "You sing and dance at your celebrations though our Holy Temple is destroyed and the city of Jerusalem is deserted!" A louder bang. "You don't study. . . ."

Esther jumped with each bang. She had never seen Uncle Amnon so angry. "Stop!" she cried. "You'll break the bench."

He stopped banging and took a deep breath. "Ouch," he said and began to rub his hand.

"We need you, Uncle Amnon," Esther blurted out quickly before he could begin shouting and banging again. "We need a kohen to redeem the baby. You would make Mama very happy."

Amnon stopped rubbing. He chewed his lip thoughtfully and wrinkled his forehead. Finally he mumbled into his beard, "Well then, I'll come. But only because the Torah tells us that we must redeem the firstborn of man. And because it will make your Mama and my wife Esther happy."

"And me too," Penina laughed.

* * *

On the afternoon of the pidyon haben oil lamps were lit in niches in the courtyard walls. The white stone of the walls and floor gleamed like gold in the lamplight. From the kitchen yard came the good smells of bread baking in the round clay oven and the sizzling sound of lamb turning slowly on a spit.

Two jugs of wine were cooling in the grape arbor where Penina sat holding the baby. A long table loaded with sweets stood behind her. She snatched a tiny, rolled raisin cake and a nut candy and stuffed them in her mouth. The table was piled so high with plums, pomegranates, honey cakes, and other good things that even her sharp-eyed mother didn't notice.

"You *are* getting prettier," Penina said, looking down at the baby while she chewed. He was watching the light flicker through the grape leaves and waved one tiny arm to catch the sunbeams.

"Don't worry about today, baby," Penina whispered. "A pidyon haben isn't like a berit milah. It won't hurt. Uncle Amnon will hold you for a minute and pretend that he's taking you to be a servant in the Temple. Then your father Mosheh will pay Uncle Amnon five coins to buy you back. Then you'll be free again."

The baby turned his blue-gray eyes to Penina's face as if he were listening to every word. She hugged him and rocked and waited happily for Uncle Amnon and Aunt Esther to arrive.

Guests stepped out of litters at the gate and bustled in, tinkling and sparkling in their earrings, necklaces, jeweled headdresses, and sequined scarves. They "oohed" and "aahed" over the guest of honor, the firstborn son. But the baby snuggled deeper into Penina's arms, curled his small legs against her bright sash, and fell asleep.

In the twilight the lamps glowed more brightly and the courtyard grew cooler. The chatter of the guests grew livelier and louder—and then suddenly it quieted. Penina looked up and saw Amnon and Esther standing at the gate. They wore simple, dark, woolen robes and head coverings, without jewelry or perfumes. They looked with disapproval at the brightly dressed guests and the tables loaded with sweets.

"Amnon, Esther," Penina's mother cried happily. She rushed to greet them and pulled them to the arbor to see the baby and his parents. Amnon's face softened, and he smiled at Penina and stroked the sleeping baby's cheek.

The baby slept on as the guests gathered around the arbor and the ceremony began. The infant's father, Mosheh, placed the baby on an embroidered, damask pillow and handed the baby on the pillow to Amnon the kohen. In a loud, firm voice he said, "This, my firstborn, is the firstborn of his mother. The Holy One, blessed be He, has commanded us to redeem him."

Amnon asked gravely, "Would you rather give him to me or would you rather redeem him for five shekels as the Torah requires?"

"I would rather redeem my son," answered Mosheh quickly, "and here is the value of his redemption as the Torah requires."

Amnon took the coins and gave the baby back to his father. Then, placing the coins on the baby's forehead, Amnon recited prayers of hope that the little one would grow up to do good deeds, to raise a family, and to follow the laws of the Torah.

Penina looked across at Aunt Esther and her mother who stood side by side, and she smiled. "I did it," she thought proudly. "I brought the whole family together and made everybody happy."

As Amnon finished the prayers, Penina's mother filled a cup with wine. "For the final blessing," she said, handing it to the kohen.

Amnon pushed the cup away in horror and stepped back. "No! I can't drink wine while the Temple lies in ruins."

Mosheh was equally horrified. "Won't you recite the blessing and drink in honor of my son?"

"No. It is forbidden. How can we enjoy meat and wine and celebrate with music and parties when we are exiled from the Land of Israel?"

"That's Karaite nonsense," Mosheh said roughly. "Rabbi Joshua tells us in the Talmud that we may feast and build homes and live good lives even in exile, as long as we don't forget the Temple."

Amnon turned red again. He shouted, "Rabbi Joshua—pteh!" He spat on the white stone floor of the courtyard. Angry murmurs rose from the other guests, but Amnon shouted above them, "You follow the rabbis like sheep. The rabbis make up new rules to make life easy in exile. But their rules are lies! There is only one truth—the truth of the Torah, which is the word of God!"

"Do you dare to insult the Talmud?" Mosheh roared, leaning forward and forgetting the baby in his arms. The baby trembled, woke, and began to howl, kicking his legs in Mosheh's face.

Penina's mother snatched the baby as the two men glared, almost nose to nose, with their beards thrusting at each other like bristly brooms.

"Heathen!" cried Mosheh.

"Sheep!" shouted Amnon. "What does a pidyon haben mean to a flock of sheep? Take back your money!" He flung the five coins of redemption

money to the ground and pushed through the crowd to reach the gate. His wife Esther hurried after him.

"Wa . . . wa . . . wa . . ." The baby's wails filled the silence.

"The poor baby," Penina cried. "He's not redeemed anymore." On her hands and knees, she scrambled between people's feet, found the coins, and raced out the gate and down the dark street.

Beyond the empty market square, she saw the bouncing light of Amnon's and Esther's small lantern. She flew after them, passed them, and turned with her arms held wide, blocking the narrow lane. "You have to take the money," she panted indignantly. "You're a kohen."

"Get out of my way," Amnon growled. "I should never have come to your heathen household. You're not Jews anymore. You're Rabbanites."

"We are too Jews. We're children of Abraham, just like you," Penina sputtered. "You have to redeem the baby!" She thrust the coins at him.

Amnon's eyes flashed in the lantern light. "You're an ignorant, disrespectful child."

"But she's right," Esther said.

He gulped deep breaths of air, and slowly his face grew calm. His eyes began to crinkle in the old, friendly way. "She's right." he repeated. He took the coins from Penina's hand. Then suddenly lifting her in a great, prickly-bearded hug, he said, "Thank you for the Torah lesson, little Pepper Pot."

CHAPTER
8

SILVER DIRHEM, c. 900
Struck in Cordova by the caliph of Spain. It
is inscribed on one side with the phrase, "There
is no God but Allah," on the other, "In the
name of Allah the Merciful."

"Cordova? Is that Babylonia too?" Sarah asked.
   "Cordova is Spain," said Grandma.
   "They sure moved around in those years. How come the Jews went to
Spain when you said they were so happy in Babylonia?" Jamie asked.
   Grandma shrugged. "Times changed. By 900 there was lots of trouble
for the Babylonians and for the Jews in Babylonia. Many Jews from North
Africa and from Babylonia moved across to Spain which became, for Jews,
a center of science, music, poetry, and religious study. This coin was struck
at the beginning of the Golden Age of Jewish life in Spain."

The Double Purim

Spain, c. 900

The storyteller whirled around the courtyard, his huge turban wobbling
and his tunic flapping in the children's faces. Suddenly he stopped, leaned
toward the brightly dressed audience, and whispered—

Our Purim tale is nearly done.
Hush now; the fun is yet to come.

The children squirmed, giggled, and then grew quiet as he continued—

The king's advisor fumed and steamed.
"I'll teach those Jews," he grimly schemed.
"If they won't bow, then they must die.
I'll chop them, lop them, hang them high!"

"Who is the advisor, children?" shouted the storyteller.
"Haman!" they shrieked back at him, waving their hamsa sugar cookies and pounding the tile floor of the courtyard.

Arieh's eyes shone, and he stamped and yelled as loudly as the little ones, but he stood in back with the adults. This was partly because he felt strange in this crowd of Spanish Jews. He and his parents had come to Cordova from Babylonia only a few weeks before. But it was also because he was almost grown up. He was twelve years old, with a shadow of a mustache on his upper lip, and he worked as an apprentice with his father, the physician Judah ibn Talfon.

He looked shyly at the bigger boys and thought, "If they play Purim games later, I'll show them some tricks with my Babylonian sheep's-knuckle dice." The dice rattled against the silver dirhem inside his robe. "It's going to be a fun night," he thought and smiled to himself.

Now the storyteller was dancing on the ledge of the fountain. He raised his hands for quiet and went on.

> Queen Esther cooked a wondrous meal.
> The king devoured it and squealed,
> "I must repay you for this feast."
> "Please do," she said. "Just hang that beast!"

"Which beast, children?" the storyteller bellowed the question.

"Haman!" Children and adults together roared the answer, stamping and whistling until the flames of the oil lamps whipped about and the lemons on the courtyard trees bobbed up and down.

Again the storyteller raised his arms. But the noise went on until he pulled off his huge turban, dipped it in the fountain and splashed the children. There were more shrieks and tumbling about until finally they began to quiet down. It was then that everybody heard loud knocking at the courtyard gate.

Eliezer the gatekeeper shuffled over and peered through the grill. He jumped back, raised the bar, and swung the gate wide. Four men, wearing the green cloaks of the caliph's guards and carrying blazing torches, stood in the entrance. "Swine!" barked the leader. "How do you dare to keep the caliph's men waiting? The caliph requires the services of the Babylonian physician Judah ibn Talfon—immediately!"

Arieh's father sprang up even before the soldier finished speaking. He threw off his bright holiday robe and slipped into the black cloak that Arieh's mother brought. Arieh leaped over the children in front and ran into the library where scrolls of Talmud lay on shelves on one side of the room and scrolls of medicine on the other. He brought out his father's leather case, filled with salves, medicines, and tools.

"God be with you," murmured his mother as the father and son hurried out of the warm, festive courtyard into the dark street.

Arieh had to run to keep up with the men, and the bag bounced against his legs. He looked up and saw his father's lips moving, murmuring in Hebrew, "Dear God, make my hands quick and gentle and my eyes and mind sharp so that I may serve the caliph. And protect me from my enemies."

"What enemies, Papa?" Arieh asked in a whisper. "How can we have enemies already? We just got here."

"If the caliph wants a new physician, his own doctors must have failed him. The caliph's regular physicians will be my enemies tonight," Judah answered grimly.

They moved under an arch into a cool, sweet-smelling garden. On the opposite side another archway led them into a long, lamplit passage and then into a large room. A fat, red-faced man lay groaning on a couch at the far end. Two turbaned slaves watched over him silently.

Judah stopped before the couch and bowed. Arieh bowed too. They could see that the caliph's throat and jaw were purple and horribly swollen. "Like a bullfrog," Arieh thought, but he quickly squelched the disrespectful idea.

The caliph raised a limp hand. "You are the Jewish physician from Baghdad?" he asked in a weak, husky voice.

"Yes, Excellency."

"Then cure me, unbeliever! These Muslim fools are worthless."

Two black-robed men stirred uneasily in the shadows by the door, but they said nothing. As Judah began to examine the sick man, they moved closer and watched. On a low bench Arieh laid out the tools and medicines from the bag. Then his father signaled him to bring an oil lamp close and raise it high.

Judah murmured to himself as he carefully prodded the swollen area and felt the burning heat of the sick man's body. "Infection and fever . . . an incision right here . . . drain . . ."

The Cordova physicians moved even closer, watching eagerly and suspiciously.

"Your Excellency," Judah said at last, "your fever is caused by fluid which fills your throat and jaw. It must be drawn out. With your permission, I want you to drink this juice of the poppy to ease your pain. Then I will begin to draw the fluid."

"W-will you cut?" The caliph's voice shook.

"A small incision is needed to allow the fluid to leave."

"Hear me, Jew," the weak voice rasped. "If you fail, your throat will be cut and your infidel tongue will be silenced forever!"

Arieh shivered, but Judah calmly held the poppy juice to the caliph's lips and then stepped back and waited.

Slowly the caliph's body relaxed, and his eyes closed. Arieh moved closer and held the lamp so that it shone on the swollen area. With a tiny knife his father cut lightly across the highest point of the swelling. A line of red appeared. Arieh saw the two slaves stir and tighten like big cats preparing to spring. His father's fingers moved over the swelling, pressing the liquid toward the opening. More bright blood appeared.

"Useless," growled one of the Cordova doctors. He was standing at Arieh's elbow.

"Stupid," agreed the other.

The long fingers kept pressing gently, firmly, patiently.

Long moments passed. Arieh could hardly breathe in the tense silence until, suddenly, a blob of greenish pus appeared at the cut and began to ooze out.

There was a gasp and a sharp movement behind Arieh. A black-sleeved arm struck his elbow. The lamp tipped and hot oil poured out onto his hand and wrist. Pain tore through his arm and his whole body. He forced his left hand up to support the lamp, bit his lips to keep from crying out, and willed himself to stand firm.

A slave leaped forward with his dagger drawn and pounced on the doctor beside Arieh. But Arieh didn't hear the doctor cry out. He was fighting to hold back tears at the burning pain in his arm, and he was silently repeating again and again, "Hold the lamp steady, hold the lamp steady. . . ."

Minutes or hours later, Arieh didn't know how long, he felt the lamp being pried out from between his fingers. He settled slowly onto the bench. The fire in his hand and wrist began to cool as his father spread salve over them. As the physician worked, he recited the Gomel, the prayer of thanks to God at being saved from great danger. "You were very brave, my son," he said when he was finished. He looked anxiously into Arieh's eyes. "Can you walk?"

Arieh nodded.

Judah turned to the slaves. "The caliph will sleep till morning," he said. "I'll come back to care for him at dawn. Guard his rest. Don't let anybody disturb him."

The slaves scowled and nodded, squeezing the handles of their daggers.

The physicians of Cordova had disappeared.

Arieh leaned on his father, and they went out through the passageway, through the sweet-smelling garden, and into the street. A slave carrying a torch led the way.

"Why did the doctor push me?" Arieh asked. "Did he want to kill the caliph?"

"It might have been an accident. Or maybe he wanted to stop me, to destroy me before I could take his place," Judah said. "You made this a double Purim, my son. Your steady hand may have saved our people just as Esther once did. If you had dropped the lamp—if my hand had slipped in the dark—it would have meant punishment or death for you and me. But, even worse, the caliph's soldiers might have punished all the Jews of Cordova."

"Because *we* made a mistake?"

"Because we're Jews. Even here in Spain, the kindest of all the lands of exile, the Muslims are ready to punish all Jews for the mistakes of one."

The courtyard was quiet. The Purim feast had ended long before. Arieh's mother ran to greet them. At the sight of his bandaged hand she set him down on a cushion, laid a sheepskin robe on his knees, and hurried to pour two cups of wine.

"Now tell me." She turned to her husband.

The doctor's face was pale and tired. "It was an infection that I had to lance. The caliph will recover, with God's help. I will go back to care for him at dawn," he said. "But Arieh will stay at home." He ran his hand softly over the boy's hair. "He'll tell you about his part tonight. It was a brave part."

Judah stood up and rubbed his eyes. "I have to look through the scroll of my friend Rhazes, the Baghdad physician. He writes about treatment of infected areas."

"Galen also—the scroll I translated for you from Greek into Arabic," Arieh's mother said quickly.

"Yes." Their eyes met in the look of sharing that always made Arieh jealous. They were partners and friends as well as parents. But tonight it was all right. He was a partner too. He had made that night a double Purim. He felt the dice and the silver dirhem tucked away in his robe. They'd have to wait until next Purim when his big, clumsy hand had healed.

CHAPTER

9

"Number Nine looks even stranger than the ones with Arabic writing," said Jamie.

"Mmmmm-hmmmm," said Grandma, "very, very strange. Not only is the writing strange; it also has a square hole in the middle. Let's look at the chapter on Indian coins and Chinese coins."

"Indians didn't use coins. They used wampum," Jamie said, feeling very superior.

"Indian Indians, not American Indians," Grandma said and began to clean the small, brown coin.

BRONZE CHIEN, c. 1100
Coined in China. On one side it is inscribed with the words, "The current money of the Kai Yuan period." On the other side is a raised crescent. Chien coins were strung together on a string. Sixteen coins were equal to one ounce of bronze.

"Chinese? Were there Jews in China?" Sarah asked in a surprised voice.

"There were Jews everywhere," Grandma said proudly. "The first Jews may have come to China at the time of the Maccabees. Others followed. The Jews were great traders. They carried coins and merchandise between China and many other countries of Asia, Africa, and Europe. Wherever they went, they took messages from one Jewish community to another."

The Messenger and the Monkey

Aden, c. 1100

The camels dozed under the palm trees, and the monkeys slept in their cage. But one monkey chattered mournfully. Nothing else moved on the wharf of Aden in the burning heat of midday. Then a wiry boy in a black shirt with a yellow sash at his waist—the sign of a Jew—raised his head from the shade beside the cage of monkeys. He peered out at the hazy water of the Red Sea, looking for sails.

"Maybe the ship sank in a storm. Maybe it was taken by pirates," the boy thought. He was tired of waiting. For each of the past four mornings he had carried a heavy jug of rosewater to the wharf and squatted in the shade, selling drinks to sailors while he watched the sea.

The mori, his rabbi, had given him clear instructions. "Abraham," he had said, "you must wait for a single-masted ship from Egypt. As soon as it docks, find the captain, Shimon ibn Tuviah, and bring him to me. He carries an important message from Rabbi Mosheh ben Maimon. It must not fall into the hands of the governor of Aden."

Abraham brushed away a listless fly. As he dug into his pouch and pulled out some dates and a flat bread, a long, hairy arm reached through the bamboo bars of the cage. Abraham's teeth flashed in a wide, white grin against his brown face as he shared his bread.

"Eat well, little monkey," he murmured. "Maybe you're an orphan like me. Who knows where the trader will take you, or who will buy you."

Voices and sharp commands came from the alley behind the wharf where the windowless stone warehouses of the port stood. Herbs and spices from India, silks and fine porcelain from China, and ivory from Africa were stored in these warehouses. Now six of the governor's soldiers waited in the shade of the buildings, their fingers holding tightly around the hilts of their curved swords. They stared past Abraham—out to the sea.

He looked up over the cage again and almost swallowed a date pit in his surprise. A white sail was coming up over the horizon. Within minutes the wooden hull of the ship appeared. It was low in the middle and stood high at the front and back to help the sailors fight off pirates. The ship rushed toward shore, driven by the hot wind. Soon the sail was furled, and the ship turned and slowed down until it bumped gently against the dock. Men sprang out to tie the ship fast, and sailors began to lower the gangplank. But, before they were done, a short, barrel-chested man wearing a gleaming, white turban and long, striped robe jumped nimbly from the deck to the wharf. He looked around, saw Abraham, and hurried toward him.

At that moment the governor's men came clattering onto the wharf. The man hesitated; then he seemed to stumble over a coil of rope and fall with a loud "oof." By the time he had untangled his robe and picked himself up the soldiers had reached him.

"Are you Shimon ibn Tuviah, the Jew from Egypt?" asked the officer in charge.

"I am," the man nodded.

"You are to come with us, by the order of the governor."

"It is my delight to obey every wish and command of your noble ruler," said ibn Tuviah with a deep bow, "but first I must recite the afternoon prayer as our Holy Bible and our prophet Abraham have required." Without waiting for an answer, he turned, facing north to Jerusalem, and began to rock back and forth.

Abraham squeezed himself close against the cage and waited, terrified of what would happen next. Would the soldiers slash the Jew to pieces for his insolence, or would they simply drag him off to jail?

Nothing happened. The men looked at each other uneasily and then stepped back and waited. Maybe they waited out of respect for the prophet Abraham, forefather of both Jews and Muslims, or maybe the captain's boldness had shocked them into silence. For whatever reason, the Jew prayed undisturbed.

"Baruch Atah, Adonai Elohenu, Melech ha'olam," the man sang in Hebrew. Then he continued in the same singsong with these words in Hebrew, "Jewish boy with the water jug, you will find a scroll under the rope. Take it to your rabbi. Show it to nobody else, or all of us will die." He continued to rock and sing with his eyes closed, repeating the traditional words of the prayer, "asher kideshanu bemitzvotav vetzivanu. . . ." Finally he stopped and turned to the soldiers, without even a glance at Abraham. "Lead the way," he said briskly.

Abraham watched them leave, open-mouthed with surprise. Never, never before had he seen a Jew talk back to a Muslim—and a thousand times never to soldiers of the governor. The fly buzzed around his nose and settled on his lip. Pfffzzz . . . Abraham blew him off and shut his mouth, remembering the strange words of the captain's prayer.

"Was he talking to me?" he asked himself. He looked around. The wharf was empty again. The ship from Egypt bobbed up and down beside it, and a bare-chested, black sailor sat cross-legged on the deck with a scimitar resting on his knee.

"He must've been talking to me," Abraham realized. His eyes moved to the coil of rope beside the monkey cage, the coil that the captain had stumbled over. Abraham took his jug and slid along the wharf until he was leaning against the coil. The monkey watched him with bright, curious eyes. Abraham slipped his hand under the coil and felt around. Something smooth, long, and thin rolled under his fingers. The scroll! Rabbi Maimon's scroll!

How could he get it away secretly? Abraham did the first thing that came into his mind. He tipped his jug, letting the rosewater gurgle out and under the cage of monkeys. Then he slid out the scroll and dropped it into the empty jug.

Abraham's hands were shaking. His body was sticky with sweat. "Now, back to the Jewish quarter," he told himself. He stood up and lifted the jug to his shoulder.

"Boy, I'm dry as a bone," one of the wharfmen called as he strolled toward Abraham. "Give me a drink."

Abraham looked up at the man and began to back away. "I-I-I . . . ," he stuttered, trying to think of an excuse so that he wouldn't have to tip the bottle. The man moved forward, scowling; Abraham leaped backward, crashed into the bamboo monkey cage, and fell across its top. His arms and legs thrashed as he juggled wildly to keep the water jug from falling and breaking open.

At the sudden weight, the catch on the door of the cage fell open, and the door swung out. Six delighted monkeys sprang out onto the wharf and raced off in all directions.

"Cursed of Allah, get back here!" cried the wharfman, turning and running after the nearest monkey.

"Ya, ya, cursed ones," yelled Abraham enthusiastically, clutching his jug and racing after another one. He quickly reached the alley, skidded around the corner, and headed for the Jewish quarter. The monkey followed its nose to the vegetable market.

*   *   *

One at a time the Jews of Aden slipped into the small, low-ceilinged synagogue. They found places on the floor cushions, leaned against the walls, and waited eagerly for the rabbi to read the precious scroll from Egypt. It was Mosheh ben Maimon's responsa, his long-awaited answers to the questions they had sent him. The tiny, lean rabbi cleared his throat

and raised the scroll. Suddenly, there was a loud knock on the door.

"The governor's men!" gasped the rabbi. He fled into the next room, hugging the scroll. Abraham's uncle jumped up and loudly began to chant a prayer. Abraham and the others joined in as the door opened, and Shimon ibn Tuviah strode into the room.

A hubbub of welcomes and relieved laughter filled the synagogue. "Shalom alecha . . . hallelujah . . . praise God's mercy that you were saved," people cried.

With a wide smile the sturdy captain announced, "I was saved by the mercy of God—but also by the greed of the governor. He demanded the scroll of Mosheh ben Maimon. When it could not be found, he graciously accepted in its place a jeweled Florentine dagger and a purse of Chien coins from China."

The captain settled back in the place of honor at the right hand of the rabbi. Again the rabbi cleared his throat and raised the scroll. "In our message to the great Rabbi ben Maimon," he began in a quavery voice, "we asked whether we should follow those among us who call themselves messiahs." He turned to the scroll and continued, "Rabbi Maimon, our teacher, answers, 'No. You must not follow them. They are false or misguided men. The time of the true Messiah has not yet come. The false messiahs may anger the caliph and the other rulers. Then terrible punishment will come down on the heads of all Jews.' "

The rabbi's voice softened to a whisper as he read the next words, "Our rulers oppress us cruelly because we are Jews. But we know that their religion is no more than an imitation of our true religion and their prophet is no more than a madman."

The listeners shuddered, and anxious eyes looked to the doors and windows.

"We are God's chosen people," the rabbi read on. His voice grew louder and trembled with pride and joy. "We will outlive all of our tormenters. We must be brave, faithful, and patient. The true Messiah will soon come."

Abraham could feel his uncle straighten up beside him. The other men's eyes brightened. As they listened, they forgot that as Jews they had to pay special taxes, to wear ugly, black clothing with yellow belts, to walk in the gutter, to bow down to any Muslim, and to suffer a thousand other insults. God was with them. They could wait patiently and proudly for God's Messiah to redeem them.

But Abraham fidgeted. He braided and unbraided the fringes of his shirt and stared across at the captain. Ibn Tuviah sat erect, listening closely with his arms crossed on his chest.

"I want to be like him," Abraham thought. "I don't want to creep around with a bent back while I wait for the Messiah."

The captain's eyes met his. They twinkled as ibn Tuviah recognized the boy who had helped him on the wharf, and the captain nodded a greeting.

"Now we will feast to honor our guest from Egypt," Abraham's uncle called out when the reading was finished. Straw mats were laid on the earthen floor. Bowls filled with vegetables and tiny pieces of mutton and trays heaped with flat breads were placed on the mats. The people sat together, scooping tidbits from the bowls onto chunks of bread, laughing and discussing Rabbi Maimon's warm, brotherly message. Every few minutes, as their happiness overflowed, they stopped to sing psalms, clap, and snap their fingers.

For Abraham the best part of the feast began when ibn Tuviah belched gently, settled back against the wall, and began to tell about his travels.

"I do God's holy work, and I serve myself at the same time," he said.

"I sail toward the rising sun, carrying pearls from the Red Sea to the lords of China and fine damascus swords to the princes of India. And I bring messages and the responsa of the rabbis to the Jews of all the lands I reach in my travels." He leaned forward, speared a bit of mutton on his dagger, and continued, "On my way back I carry perfumes, spices, porcelain, and silk to the pale nobles of Spain and France. To the rabbis I bring questions of law from the Jews of the East.

"It's a free life but a hard and dangerous one. Many a captain has had his head lopped off by pirates or by greedy noblemen. Many a ship and crew have gone down in a wild storm."

He sighed and laid down his knife before he continued, "But the loneliness I feel on these long trips is worse than the danger. If I had a son to share my work, a boy to sit and study Torah with me when the sea is calm, then I would be content. A boy like the quick-witted one on the wharf who heard my prayer and saved the scroll."

"That's me!" Abraham jumped up excitedly. He quickly sat down, embarrassed, as everybody stared at him.

But Abraham's uncle twirled his earlock thoughtfully and nodded. "The hand of God may be in this," he said. "The boy is an orphan. The governor of Aden has the right to take him away from us and raise him as a Muslim. If Abraham is willing to go with you, Shimon ibn Tuviah, he will be safe from the danger of being converted to Islam."

"I'm willing, I'm willing!" Abraham jumped up again.

"Then we've made a match!" cried ibn Tuviah.

*   *   *

The wailing call of the muezzin hadn't yet sounded to call the Muslims to predawn prayer when Abraham and ibn Tuviah hurried to the wharf. House windows were shuttered, and the alleys were dark. But, as they passed the stone warehouses, a hairy, shivering little body sprang from a roof ledge. It landed with a thump on Abraham's back and wound long arms and legs around him.

"What?" muttered ibn Tuviah and grasped his dagger.

"No. Stop! It's my friend," Abraham whispered urgently. "He helped me save the scroll."

The captain chuckled. "God sends strange and unexpected helpers," he murmured. "Bring him along."

Abraham coaxed the monkey around and nested him inside his shirt. Then they hurried across the wharf and climbed the gangplank.

• • •

While Sarah finished drawing the bronze Chien, Jamie counted on his fingers. His eyes grew wider and wider as he bent each finger down. "I can't believe it!" he said finally. "We just went through 2,600 years, twenty-six centuries."

Grandma took off her glasses and rubbed her eyes. "No wonder I'm starting to see double."

"We'll come back tomorrow to do the next 800 years," Jamie said. "What kind of cookies will you have?"

"To get us through 800 years we'll need chocolate chips," said Grandma.

"Yippee!" both children cheered.

*   *   *

The smell of freshly baked chocolate chip cookies filled the kitchen the next afternoon, and seven numbered coins waited on the table. Sarah and Jamie piled their books on the washing machine and got ready for work. First they would finish the cookies and then the coins.

With a mouthful of cookies Sarah mumbled, "The coins are very interesting, but so far . . ."

"Chew and swallow, then talk," said Grandma.

Sarah chewed and gulped and said, ". . . but so far we don't know any more about Uncle Otto than we did 2,600 years ago when we identified the little horse's head."

Grandma sighed and nodded. "So far you're right, but be patient. Someplace in this pile of coins we'll find a clue to Uncle Otto's secret. I can feel it in my bones."

75

CHAPTER
10

"Do your bones feel anything special about Numbers Ten and Eleven, Grandma?" Sarah asked.

"They are shiny yellow. That means they're gold," Jamie said. "And Number Ten has that squirly Arabic writing on it." He was starting to feel like a coin expert as he skimmed through the pages of Arab coins. Before Sarah could finish drawing, Jamie had identified Number Ten.

GOLDEN SEQUIN, c. 1550
Coined in Constantinople, Turkey. It is inscribed with the name and the many titles of the sultan, Suleiman I.

"Turkey! Gobble, gobble." Jamie started flapping his arms and hopping around the kitchen. He stopped to dip into the cookie jar and came hopping back with a cookie for Sarah. She chewed thoughtfully and then asked, "Why did the Jews go to Turkey? Our last coin was from China, and two coins ago the Jews were in Spain. Why did they move around so much?"

"That's what I asked a few centuries ago when they skipped from Babylonia to Spain," said Jamie.

"There was always a good reason to move on," Grandma said. "The Jews were more or less happy and secure in Spain while it was ruled by both Muslims and Christians. But, when the Christians drove out all the Muslims, the Christians also forced the Jews to leave, or to become Christians. Jews fled to Turkey, North Africa, even to America. Some went on from Turkey to settle in Palestine, the Promised Land."

"So this golden sequin might even be from Palestine," Sarah said.

Even God Has to Be Fair

Safed, c. 1550

Skwitch . . . skwitch . . . skwitch . . . Grazia squeezed the goat's teats and warm milk squirted into the clay basin. The little, brown and white kid butted at her side, waiting to drink.

"All right, little greedy one." Grazia picked up the basin and made room for the kid. "Mama," she called into the house, "we got even less milk today than yesterday."

"It's the drought." Her mother looked up from her weaving and sighed. "The poor goats aren't getting enough water to drink."

"And Mama, Spotty, the little kid, is getting skinnier and skinnier. Maybe we shouldn't take so much milk from its mother."

Grazia's mother came to the door and squinted into the cold, glaring sunlight. "Then how will we make cheese? And what will you and your little brother eat? What's more important, a baby goat or a human being?"

"A baby goat," Grazia laughed. But she was only half-joking as she fondly petted the kid's soft, spotted coat.

Her mother shook her head. "This Land of Israel is a hard land," she said. "It's already past Tu Bishvat, and we've had no rain. Even the olive trees are dropping leaves, and their roots are searching deep, deep in the earth for water." As she turned back to her loom, she called, "Bring in the milk, then come help me wind the wool."

Inside, the small room with its whitewashed, stone walls was even colder than the yard. Grazia's mother pulled her shawl close. "In Smyrna, where your father and I grew up, the fields were always green, and the fig trees were sprouting new leaves by this time of year," she said.

"Then why did you and Papa come here to Safed?"

"Because it's the Holy Land, child! It's God's commandment that we should live here. When the Messiah comes, all the Jews will return to the Land of Israel. But those who died and were buried far away will have to roll under the oceans and the mountains to get here."

Grazia shivered to think of all those poor, rolling Jews. But her mother was worrying again about the rain. "If no rain falls now in the winter to fill the cistern under the house, what will we use for drinking and cooking in the summertime? And where will we get water and grass for the goats?"

"Yehudit, Grazia!" A shout from the yard interrupted them. Grazia's

father pushed open the door, letting in a blast of cold wind. His face was pale from long hours of study in the synagogue, and he was as thin as Spotty the goat, but his eyes shone with excitement. "Come with me. Dress warmly and bring the baby. The rabbi is leading all the children to the top of the hill to pray for rain. He had a sign from heaven. In his prayers this morning he heard over and over, 'God will have pity on the children.' Hurry!"

Yehudit tucked the drowsy baby under her shawl as she, Grazia, and Grazia's father went quickly along the narrow, cobblestone streets to Rabbi Nathan's synagogue. Spotty trotted happily along beside them. A crowd of children was already huddled by the stone steps that led down to the entrance, and curious Muslim neighbors watched from their balconies. Grazia heard the earnest drone of men's voices at prayer in the dark room below.

"Hey, goat-girl, I bet your goat prays better than you do," called freckled

Benjamin, the boy who lived next door. He was Grazia's special enemy because he always teased her and pulled her braids. The boys standing with him snickered and poked each other.

Grazia stuck out her tongue at Benjamin while she tried to think of an insulting answer. But a stern look from her mother silenced her.

The heavy, wooden door opened slowly. White-bearded Rabbi Nathan and two other rabbis climbed slowly up the steps, each carrying a Torah whose bells and silver crowns jingled in the cold wind. The children and parents followed them slowly up the street to the end of town.

"God of Israel, save us please. God of mercy, help us please," Rabbi Nathan called as they came out onto the rustling, tossing grass at the top of the hill. Beside a large boulder they stopped and, all together, sang psalms in praise of God. The words were snatched out of their mouths by the wind and seemed to swirl around and around the hilltop like the dry dust.

"God, give us rain," cried Rabbi Nathan in a shaking voice. "Give us rain for the sake of the children. They don't understand the difference between a God who gives rain and a God who does not."

"Give us rain, God," the children cried. And Grazia warmed her hands against Spotty's warm, little body and added, "For us and for Spotty too."

"I see it coming!" cried Benjamin. "There—over the sheikh's house."

Dark clouds were moving toward them over the mountains. "Rain, rain!" the children yelled happily. Grazia lifted her face to the sky to catch the first drops. The rabbis sang on, but they peeked up at the clouds through their bushy eyebrows while the wind ripped at their robes and at the Torahs they carried.

The black clouds were rushing toward them as if all the devils of hell were chasing them. They filled the sky overhead and darkened the hilltop. In a moment they would open and let the rain fall. But the wild wind wouldn't let them rest. It drove them with fierce gusts until they moved on, carrying their blessed rain away from the thirsty town of Safed. The sky brightened, the wind died, and the cold, hateful sun began to shine again. And the rabbis with the jingling Torahs, the children, parents, and Spotty the goat started sadly down the hill again.

Grazia slipped her hand into her father's. "Why won't God send rain, Papa?" she asked.

"Because our sins are great. We are not following God's laws," Grazia's father answered.

"But Papa, you study and pray all the time. And Mama is always spinning and weaving and taking care of us. How can you be bad?" She thought a minute. "Maybe it's me. Is God angry because I tripped Benjamin and made him fall on his face after he pulled my hair?"

Her father smiled. "That wasn't a good thing to do, but I don't think it has anything to do with the rain."

"Then God has no good reason. And, if God has no good reason, God shouldn't stop the rain. It's not fair!"

"Grazia Shulamit bat Yehudit," said her father, calling her by her full name, which was a sure sign that he was angry, "We Jews do not curse God when bad things happen. When good comes, a Jew thanks God; when bad comes, he thanks God too! Now go and help your mother and stop asking silly questions. I'm going back to the synagogue."

"But you haven't eaten," said Grazia's mother.

"I'll fast to clear my mind. And I'll search the holy books. Someplace there is a magic combination of Hebrew letters that can rise up to heaven, right to the seat of the Almighty. God must hear our prayers—not just to bring rain, but to bring the Messiah, to save the world."

* * *

After her lunch of bread, olives, and cheese, Grazia sat in the chilly sunlight of the yard, thinking very hard while she shelled almonds. Every now and then she let a nut drop for Spotty.

"Papa says, if we can put Hebrew letters in the right order, they'll carry a message up to heaven," she thought. "But the trouble is that nobody knows the right order." The pile of shells grew . . . and, suddenly, as Grazia looked at them she had a wonderful idea. "God knows the right order," she thought. "I'll ask God to help me." She gathered some shells in her skirt, took a blackened twig from the fire, and ran inside to where her father's books stood on a shelf. Using the twig she carefully copied letters from the book covers onto the shells. Then she ran back outside and threw them into the air, yelling as loudly and quickly as she could, "Dear God, please put the letters in the right magic order, and please make it rain, and please, please save Spotty."

The shells dropped, but the sky stayed blue. And, from the roof of the next house, a voice snickered, "Please, please save Spotty."

"Ooh, I hate you!" Grazia screeched and flung all the remaining shells at her enemy, Benjamin.

* * *

The next day, when Grazia's father came wearily into the house, he told his wife, "We have to prepare for the worst. There may not be any rain this winter. We won't starve because we have a little money to buy grain. This morning Rabbi Nathan gave out the chalukah, the charity money that was sent to us by Jews in the galut." He pulled a golden sequin and a few copper coins out of his pouch and gave them to her.

"This will be only enough for us and for one or two of the milk goats," she said.

"What about Spotty?" Grazia was suddenly terrified.

"I'm afraid we'll have to butcher the young goats."

"No!" cried Grazia.

"Grazia, your little goat will die soon anyway. There won't be enough leaves and grass for it to eat this summer," said her mother. "If we butcher it now, at least we'll get some meat."

"No, no, no!" Grazia jumped up. She raced out to the yard, seized Spotty's halter, and ran with it up the dusty street.

"Is Satan chasing you, goat-girl?" Benjamin teased as she passed him.

She didn't answer, running higher and higher until she reached the bare rock where they had prayed the day before. The kid began to nose around for grass, but Grazia leaned panting against the sun-warmed surface. "You're not being fair, God," she sputtered. "Even if we do bad things, You shouldn't punish us all the time. Papa says You love us just as we love You. But I'm not so sure. And, besides, why should my little Spotty be punished and butchered? What bad thing did it ever do?"

A veil of haze began to move over the sun, and the wind was gusting again. It was getting colder. "Come on, Spotty." Grazia pulled at the goat. "God isn't listening. We have to find someplace to hide you." She began to pick her way down the steep trail that led into the valley.

Soon they were in the shade with rough, rock walls rising around them. The wind was howling more and more loudly up above, but below there were only whirlpools of breeze that shook the leathery, little oaks and rustled through the biting thistle. It was getting darker, but Spotty clattered easily from rock to rock, pulling Grazia along.

Where could they go? She was afraid to stay out. Jackals and snakes and wild boars roamed the hills. Demons and evil spirits too. Then she remembered a small Muslim village a little further along in the valley. Should she dare look for a home for Spotty there?

With a last leap the two runaways landed on the hard, red soil of the valley floor. Grazia turned fearfully and headed toward the village. The howling from above had become louder and more shrill, like the screams of dybbuks—lost, wandering souls who may not enter heaven or hell.

Grazia shivered. "Maybe we should go home," she thought. She looked up but couldn't see the path. The valley was closed in with gray-green clouds that were creeping down the rocky walls. Suddenly a flash of lightning stabbed through. For an instant the rocks were a bright blue-white. Then thunder crashed. The valley floor jumped beneath them, and Grazia fell against a bush, hugging the trembling little goat. "God of Abraham, Isaac, and Jacob, and Sarah, Rivkah, Leah, and Rachel too, I didn't mean to insult You," she called in a shaking voice. "Don't send the prince of demons down on me, please."

Lightning crashed again, and thunder rolled through the valley. As the bushes tossed, dark shapes flickered on the slopes. Already Grazia felt cold, devil fingers dancing over her hair and neck and back. They were making splotching, lip-smacking noises all around her.

"Go away!" she cried and felt for the amulet inscribed with Hebrew words that hung from her neck. It would protect her from evil spirits. The amulet felt wet and slippery. Could it be blood? Her hair was wet too. Sweet, fresh water was running into her eyes and nose. The splotching, smacking noise of the demon fingers had become the drumming of rain.

Seconds later the rain was splashing down the mountainside and swirling through the narrow valley. Spotty struggled to its feet, tugging Grazia along. It scrambled up the rocks. Grazia tried to follow but slid back. The rope slipped from her fingers. "Meh-eh-eh," the little goat bleated pitifully, waiting. Grazia grabbed at the rock but slid back again. The rushing water swept her to her knees.

Then, through the pounding of rain and the howling of wind, came a cry. It was hateful Benjamin's voice yelling, "Grazia, Grazia, where are you?"

"Here in the valley," she yelled back, spraying water out of her nose and mouth.

Moments later she saw Benjamin's striped tunic shine against the wet rocks beside the little goat. Then he was reaching toward her, pulling her up from the streaming valley floor.

"Your parents are searching for you all over Safed. They're so scared. And then I remembered that you and your goat passed me on the way up to the big rock. I thought of the path and figured you'd do something silly—so I came running."

"Silly?" she sputtered indignantly. "If it wasn't for me, it still wouldn't be raining. You, you dumbhead! I ought to trip you again."

"If you trip me again, I'll dunk you back down!"

They glared at each other with water streaming down their faces. Then Grazia burst out laughing. For once she was too tired and happy and grateful to argue.

CHAPTER
11

GOLD COIN, c. 700
Minted in Axum, Ethiopia. On one side appears
a king, seated on a throne, holding a scepter.
On the other side there is a cross surrounded
by a wreath. It is inscribed, "Israel, King of
Axum."

"That's strange," said Grandma. "This coin is Number Eleven, so it should be closer to our time than Number Ten was. Instead, the coin book says it was made many years earlier."

"There's a hole in it." Sarah pointed to the edge of the coin. "Maybe somebody who lived closer to our time found an old coin and wore it as a necklace. Then, when the coin collector got it, he dated it for the time when it was worn instead of the earlier time when it was made."

"Maybe," said Grandma doubtfully. "We'll never know for sure. But we do know that Jews lived in Ethiopia in 700 and much earlier too. And they still live there today. For many years they were cut off from other Jewish communities and thought they were the only Jews left in the world."

"Feeling all alone must've been hard," Jamie said. He ran his finger around the rim of the golden coin. "I know how that feels. There are only two other Jewish kids in my class, and, at Christmastime when everybody is excited about the holiday, we feel kind of alone."

"Oh, Jamie, that's not the same thing!" Sarah scoffed.

Jamie shrugged, but he warmed the small coin in his hand for a while before putting it down.

Asa and the Stranger

Ethiopia, 1600

"So I'm scared," Asa argued with himself, "but there's nothing I can do about it. That stupid ox, Mulu, is bigger than I am. He'll jump on me and hit me and yell, 'Ayhud-Buda-Baby-Eater,' and the people in the marketplace will just smile and turn away."

Asa raised his thin shoulders and tucked his short-cropped, black head down between them, as though he expected a blow that very minute. But his dark, lean legs kept moving down the mountain path toward the village in the valley.

His donkey plodded along behind him, carrying a heavy load of harness buckles, plough blades, knives, axes, and one huge, ancient sword with a matching shield—all newly repaired by Asa's father, the local blacksmith.

Asa and his family lived high on a mountain ridge near the mouth of

an old iron mine. Asa's aunts and uncles and other families of Beta Yisrael lived in a tiny village nearby. But only non-Jews lived in the big village in the valley.

The tiny village was Asa's second home. At holiday time and during rainy, blustery winter days, Asa and his family crossed from their ridge to his uncle's house. The Beta Yisrael families would huddle around the charcoal fire, listening as toothless Grandma Buta told about the beautiful Queen of Sheba and King Solomon of Israel—of how they met, loved each other, and had a son who became the forefather of all Beta Yisrael. Then Uncle Alibal, with his eyes flashing, would wave his walking stick dangerously as he described the glorious days when the great Jewish Queen Yehudit united all the Beta Yisrael and crushed their enemies.

Asa would smile and nod proudly with the others. But sometimes he had troubling thoughts. "Why are we so few now? Why do the others laugh at Queen Yehudit and call her 'Yudit-Budit, Baby-Eater'? Why do they force us to live in the mountains where there is no soil for farming? Why must we be blacksmiths? Why is it so hard to be Beta Yisrael?— Why, why?"

He didn't ask his hardworking parents such questions. From early morning until dusk, each day except Shabbat, the blacksmith's hammer clanged. On most days Asa, crouching beside his father, pumped the goatskin bellows to keep the charcoal hot and soften the metal. But, on market days like this one, Asa's younger sister took over the bellows, and ten-year-old Asa climbed down the steep trail to bring the finished work to the village and to collect new work.

It was the worst day of the week because thick-shouldered Mulu, the carpenter's son, Mulu the ox, was always waiting for him.

The trail was becoming broader and flatter as Asa and the donkey approached the village. Green patches of chickpeas grew in the red earth of the valley, and lacy mimosa bushes swayed behind them. A band of baboons looked up from their chickpea breakfast and hooted at him. "Hoot-hoooot!" he shouted back at them. "Lucky baboons. You have rich, red earth, and we have only the rocks of the mountaintop. It's because we're weak," he thought to himself, "because there are so few of us. I wish we weren't alone."

Asa's bare feet and the donkey's sharp, little hooves splashed across the stream at the edge of the village. On his way back he would stop here to wash. His father had taught him this rule the first time he came down to the village. "After being with non-Jews, a member of Beta Yisrael

must wash thoroughly," he had said. "It's hard to be of Beta Yisrael,"
Asa thought.

The cone-shaped roofs of the mud and straw houses of the village poked
above the bushes ahead. Asa took a deep breath and squared his shoulders.
As he led his donkey into the narrow path that twisted between the houses,
he watched fearfully for his enemy, Mulu. But the path was empty except
for chickens pecking in the dust and a few napping goats. A hum of voices
rose from the market. When Asa came into the sunny clearing, he saw a
crowd of villagers and a great caravan of donkeys and mules gathered at
the opposite side of the square, in the shade of a clump of baobab trees.

"Mulu must be there too. Maybe he won't see me," Asa thought, hurrying
to deliver the repaired tools to Faro the potter, old Tedessa the weaver,
and other customers. As Asa loaded new work into his patient donkey's
baskets, Tedessa asked, "Have you seen the new trader? Go and look—
you won't believe your eyes. In all my years I have never, never seen
such a trader."

Asa's curiosity won out over his fear of Mulu. After tying the donkey
to a bush, Asa ran across the square. He heard excited comments from
the villagers. He edged around the crowd and dropped to his hands and
knees to catch sight of glittering beads and knives, brightly striped cloth,
and shiny metal bowls spread on the colored mats. "A king's treasure,"
Asa marveled and tried to move closer. But suddenly a heavy hand shoved
him down onto his stomach. He felt himself being dragged backward
out of the crowd.

"Ayhud-Buda!" Mulu's voice bellowed. "Baby-Killer!" Fists pounded
Asa's back and neck as the boy curled up into a ball. With delighted
yelps Mulu's brothers jumped in to help. Asa rolled in the dust with his
eyes squeezed shut, tasting salty blood. He couldn't fight them . . . there
were too many . . . they were too big. . . .

Suddenly a deep voice thundered, "Stop! If you kill the blacksmith's
boy, how will I get my harness buckle fixed?"

The blows stopped. Even the murmur of villagers' voices stopped. It
was very quiet. Asa dared open his eyes a crack. "Yiii!" he cried out and
shut them quickly again.

A frightening creature was leaning over him. It looked like a man, but
its colors were all wrong. Its skin was pink as a lizard, its eyes the color
of the summer sky, and a great, curly beard, reddish-brown like cinnamon
bark, sprouted from its chin.

"Don't be frightened, boy," said the creature. "I'm a man, just like you, even though my skin is white. What's your name?"

"Ayhud," shouted Mulu eagerly, standing at the man's side. "He's a devil! His people suck the blood of babies and women!"

Asa struggled to get up. "That's not true," he gasped.

"Ayhud?" The stranger looked at Asa sharply. "Ayhud," the man repeated. The sky-blue eyes opened wide. "What do your people call themselves?" he asked.

Asa remembered to cover his mouth politely with his robe before he answered, "Beta Yisrael."

"Do you pray to a god?" the trader asked.

Asa nodded.

"Which way do you face when you pray?"

"To Jerusalem, the holy city."

The trader leaned closer, and his blue eyes seemed to bore into Asa's brown ones as he asked, "What do you do on the seventh day of the week?"

"We pray, our priest reads the scrolls, and we rest. Even my donkey and my uncle's slave rest on the Sabbath."

"Yes, yes." The trader's beard wiggled as he bobbed his head up and down excitedly. "And on the Passover?"

Asa gulped anxiously before answering. The trader's face frightened him. It was becoming even more pink. Only birds or flowers or the rear ends of baboons had such a color. Asa stuttered as he answered, "W-we eat s-special bread called kita, and we kill a lamb for our feast and smear its blood on the doorpost."

"Baruch Hashem!" the trader cried. He lifted Asa to his feet and kissed him on each cheek. Then he turned to the astonished villagers and said loudly, "This boy is my brother. His people are a lost tribe of my people, the people of Israel. We are as many as the sands of the desert, scattered over the whole world."

Asa wiped his bleeding nose on his fist and looked up at the strange man. "How could he be of Beta Yisrael? Everybody knows that Beta Yisrael are black, and we are all alone."

The pink-faced man turned back to Asa and asked eagerly, "Where do your people come from?"

Asa looked warily across at Mulu before he answered. But Mulu's big hands were hanging limp, and he was staring open-mouthed at the trader. "Our Bible tells us that we came from the Land of Israel, and one day God will bring us back to the land."

The man's blue eyes grew bright and wet and then overflowed. "He's crying," Asa thought with surprise, "just like my mother cries when our kohen reads about the Land of Israel."

"The Messiah will bring us all back from exile someday, my son," said the trader. He blew his nose and wiped his eyes. In that quiet minute

Asa gathered all his courage and asked, "Will Beta Yisrael be allowed to be farmers in the Land of Israel?"

"What a question! Of course! Farmers, poets, astronomers, traders . . . whatever we want." The trader lifted Asa in another great hug. Then he put him down and said briskly, "Can you bring your father and mother to me? I have many questions to ask them and much to tell them."

"Tomorrow at first light," Asa answered eagerly. He untied the donkey. Then, remembering his job, he asked, "Did you need a harness buckle repaired?"

The man smiled. He took the broken buckle from his saddlebag and gave it to Asa. Searching in a deep pocket of his pouch, he found a shiny golden coin, which he put into Asa's hand and said, "This is a very precious, very old coin. It bears the name 'Israel,' the name of our people. Keep it and remember that you're not alone."

"We're not alone, we're not alone"—the words sang in Asa's head as he led the donkey out of the village. He repeated the words as he splashed himself clean in the icy stream and hurried up the mountain trail. And, when he reached his small, round house at the top of the ridge, he burst out with a great, happy shout, "Abbat, Eenat, we're not alone!"

CHAPTER
12

"Coin Number Twelve coming up." Jamie raised the small, brown coin high in the air and zoomed it down into Sarah's hands.

Only four more coins were left in line on the kitchen table.

Sarah was worried. "We're coming closer and closer to Uncle Otto's time," she said, "and we don't have even the tiniest clue about him."

Grandma shook her head and reached for a bagel. She always ate a bagel when she was upset.

"Cocoa, anybody?" she asked.

"Cocoa and more chocolate chips," said Sarah.

As she stood mixing the cocoa, Grandma said glumly, "Maybe we won't find any answers."

"Grandma!" Jamie and Sarah objected.

"All right, all right, I apologize," she said. "We'll find the answer even if . . . if it costs me twenty more batches of cookies!"

"And two dozen bagels," Jamie laughed.

COPPER GROSCHEN, c. 1700
Coined in Prague, Czechoslovakia. The profile
of the Austrian emperor appears on one side.
An eagle appears on the other.

"Our coins are really jumping around," Sarah said. "Turkey and Ethiopia and now Czechoslovakia."

"It's our people who are jumping around," Grandma said. "After the

Jews left Palestine, they settled all over the world, but they were forced to move from place to place because of persecution. Remember how they were expelled from Spain? Like Spain, Prague was a center of Jewish life for hundreds of years. Prague's Jews had plenty of troubles—pogroms and expulsions—but they also had great scholars and merchants, and the first Hebrew printing press in central Europe."

Goodbye, Golem

Prague, 1700

High above the Prague ghetto in the attic of the Altneu Synagogue there was a small, silent room that held a mystery. People stared up at it sometimes and wondered, "Was the giant golem still hidden up there? If the monster were asleep, covered with a tallis, would he ever wake up and come thumping down the stairs and out into the street?"

The ghetto children shrieked with delighted terror at the thought—all except nine-year-old Shloimy. "I wouldn't be scared for a minute," he boasted, sticking out his chin and turning up his round, freckled nose. "I'd say, 'Shalom, Golem, what took you so long?' After all Rabbi Loew created the golem to save the Jews when they were being attacked, right? So he is our friend. What is there to be scared about?"

The children expected Shloimy to sound cool. Nothing scared him. In school he played cards on the bench beside the study table, right under the teacher's nose. And, in the synagogue, when the kohanim covered their heads and raised their hands to bless the congregation, Shloimy wouldn't close his eyes. He stared right at them, even though everybody knew it was a sin to look, and he might be struck blind.

After services on Shabbes, he would drag his friend Yosseleh to the old cemetery to play leapfrog over the tombstones, not because he wanted to insult the dead, heaven forbid, but because it was the only place in the ghetto where he could see the sky. The ghetto houses were so tall and rickety that they leaned toward each other over the narrow streets and shut out the sun.

For Shloimy it was more fun to lie on the grass between the tumbled gravestones and watch the birds flying overhead than to sit in the stuffy schoolroom. In the cemetery he once found a baby bird that had fallen

out of its nest. Shloimy took it home and fed it bread soaked in milk until it was strong enough to fly away. Then he took it back to the cemetery and set it free.

One day Shloimy's father caught him by the end of an earlock and sat him down. "For a baby bird you have patience, for a cat and a dog you have patience, but, when it comes to studying the holy books, you behave as if a fly is biting you. Why?" he asked in despair.

Shloimy wriggled and scratched his bristly, red hair and finally said, "I get tired of sitting and studying. The letters are so little, and the books are so fat. Birds don't make me tired."

"So what if you're tired? A Jewish boy has to serve God and study Torah!"

"But, Papa, the golem served God, and he never studied a word of Torah."

"Oy vay, what shall I do with this boy?" Shloimy's father let go of the earlock to raise his hands to heaven, and Shloimy raced out the door.

During Chanukah, when the gravestones were covered with snow, Shloimy made up a new game. "Let's play heroes," he said to Yosseleh. "I'll be the golem, and you can be Judah Maccabee. We'll make caves in the snow and . . ."

"Not me," said Yosseleh. "My mother will kill me if I get my shoes and socks wet. I'm going home." He tucked his hands into his sleeves and headed for the gate.

"You're a baby—scared of your mother," Shloimy teased.

Yosseleh turned around, insulted, and yelled, "You think you're so brave, playing make-believe golem. I know something you'd never do!"

"Name it!" Shloimy challenged.

"You wouldn't dare climb up to the attic of the Altneu Synagogue and find the golem."

"Why wouldn't I? The golem doesn't scare me. He's my friend."

"You talk big, but I'll bet your Chanukah gelt against mine that you wouldn't do it."

"It's a bet," Shloimy yelled back.

"Wait a minute." said Yosseleh, afraid that he might lose this bet. "You have to prove you found him."

"Ha! Of course I'll prove it. I'll bring back his tallis," said Shloimy boldly.

The next morning, after the last worshiper had rolled up his tefillin and gone home to eat potato latkes, Shloimy slipped through the small, arched doorway that led to the attic stairs of the synagogue. Here the stair edges were sharp, not worn out by centuries of feet like the front steps of the synagogue. Maybe no feet had ever climbed up here except the golem's, Rabbi Loew's, and his own. Shloimy shivered at the thought but then took a deep breath and laughed out loud. "I'm not scared," he called up into the dark stairwell. "Not scared . . . not scared," the words came echoing back. "The golem is my friend," he called again. "My friend . . . my friend," his voice echoed.

Then there was no sound at all except for the scraping of his feet on the steps, the pat of his hand as he felt his way along the stone wall, and the jingle of the two precious Chanukah groschen in his pocket. "Yosseleh is going to be very sorry when I come down," he said aloud. He liked the sound of his voice. It kept him company. "I'll have all of his Chanukah money and all of my own. Ha! That's enough to buy a penknife with two blades."

Step—scrape, step—scrape, higher and higher, until his nose suddenly hit the wall with a thump. The stairwell had ended. A passageway lit by a narrow window led off at a right angle. Shloimy rubbed his nose, then he knelt at the window, cleared away the dust, and peered out.

He was on top of the ghetto! In an open space far below he saw the snow-covered cemetery. Jumbled, narrow rooftops leaned in around it. A belt of gray ghetto walls squeezed the cemetery and the houses tightly, cutting them off from the icy Vltava River and the domes and spires of the great city of Prague. With a swoosh, a flock of pigeons sailed past the window and out over the wall into the city. "That is where the 'others' live," Shloimy thought, "the ones who attack Jews. Long ago, when they came storming into the ghetto, the giant golem had fought them and saved the Jews."

Shloimy jumped up eagerly. "I'm coming to see you, Golem," he called. At the end of the passage more steps spiralled upward. Around and around and up Shloimy went through the dusty, silent darkness. And, as he climbed, he started to think about the great, sleeping giant. What if he was angry at being awakened? Some people, Shloimy's father for example, got grouchy when you woke them from a nap. What if the golem didn't recognize Shloimy and thought he was an enemy? Shloimy stopped, stuck out his chin, and said, "Impossible, the golem is my friend." But it was such a feeble "impossible" that it didn't even make an echo.

He might have turned back, in spite of Yosseleh and the penknife, but at that moment he saw a thin line of gray light above. He went slowly up the last few steps and found himself in front of a wooden door. From behind the door Shloimy heard a soft moaning. His hair tingled, and he felt his earlocks standing straight out. "It's j-just the w-wind," he said to himself, and forced his hand to grasp the cold door handle. But he froze as a new sound began. Something was rustling, tapping, and thumping inside. "Th-the g-golem is walking around with his tallis rustling. J-just what I w-wanted to see." Shloimy pushed down on the handle. The door swung open.

With a whirr of wings something struck him in the face, flashed away, thumped against the wall, and whirred wildly toward him again.

Shloimy dropped to his knees and covered his head with his hands. The wild whirring and thumping continued above him. Carefully, Shloimy opened one eye. He saw a small, low-ceilinged room lit by a cobweb-streaked window. One pane of the window was broken, and a beam of sunlight poked in. Suddenly a tiny, gray body flung itself against the window, bounced off, hit the wall, and then fluttered desperately around the room.

"It's a bird," Shloimy realized. "It must've gotten in through the broken window, and now it can't find its way out again. Poor little thing! It will die up here." He sat up and watched the bird, fluttering around and around in a terrified circle. "If I can cover it," thought Shloimy, "it will quiet down. Then I'll take it to the window and put it out through the broken pane."

A grayish, whitish thing was spread out on the floor in the corner. He crept to it and picked it up. It was cloth, stiff and brittle with fringes and dark stripes on each end. A heap of gray dust lay underneath it.

Shloimy stood up slowly, watching the bird. It was huddled on the stone sill with its head tucked between its wings. Its bright, frightened eyes watched him move closer. With a quick movement Shloimy dropped the cloth over the tiny body, scooped it up gently, cloth and all, and pushed it through the broken pane.

"Go, little bird! Fly!" he cried. The small, gray shape fluttered free of the cloth, hovered for a minute, and then soared away over the snowy city of Prague.

Shloimy pulled the cloth back in through the broken pane, bunched it into a ball, and stuffed it into the opening. "Now no other bird will fly in here and be trapped," he said, feeling proud and happy.

He turned back to the dark room and was halfway to the door before he remembered the golem and the bet he'd made with Yosseleh. Suddenly the good, happy feeling was gone, and he was frightened again. His eyes searched the small room. It was empty except for a cobweb-covered chair that stood by the window and, in the corner, on the floor, the heap of gray dust that was as long and high as a grave mound.

Shloimy remembered that he had pulled the cloth from that corner, and the cloth had stripes and fringes. Was it the golem's tallis? Was this pile of dust all that was left of the giant golem, the hero of the ghetto?

"Golem!" Shloimy called in a shaky voice.

The pile of dust was silent. The only sound came from the wind moaning at the window.

"But there has to be a golem," Shloimy said stubbornly, sticking out his chin. "Maybe God sent him to another town to help other Jews. He'll come back when we need him. I'm sure he will."

He looked at the crumpled tallis in the window. "I could take it down to show to Yosseleh. Then I'd be able to get the penknife with two blades. But what if a bird flew in and got trapped again?"

"Naaaa, who cares about a penknife?" He shook his unruly, red hair. "Birds are more important."

Shloimy closed the wooden door behind him and started down the dark, circular staircase. "Goodbye, Golem, wherever you are," he called out.

CHAPTER 13

ZOLOTA, silver alloy, c. 1750
Coined in Constantinople, Turkey, and used
throughout the Turkish provinces, including
Morocco. Like most Islamic coins it does not
use pictures but is inscribed with the name
of the sultan.

"How did we get back to Turkey?" Jamie asked. "I thought we were just in Europe."

"Most of the Jews in the world lived in Europe by the 1700s," said Grandma, "but many also lived in Arabic-speaking lands. Some had been there since Roman times, and some came after being driven out of Spain. They had a rich Jewish culture and spoke Jewish languages that were a mixture of Arabic and Hebrew or Spanish and Hebrew.

Moussa Ibn Dayyan Helps Out

Morocco, 1800

A strange hiccuping sound woke Naima. She stared into the darkness and listened. At first there were only the usual wheezings and snorts from her five younger brothers who were curled together like puppies on the

99

mat nearby. And then she heard it again—a choked sob right beside her. Could it be her older sister?

"Hey, Ruhama, you're getting my back wet. Why are you crying?" she whispered.

Without answering, Ruhama thumped onto her other side to face the mud brick wall, but her shoulders kept shaking.

"Is it because of the wedding?" Naima guessed. "Are you scared?"

Ruhama got very quiet.

"She's holding her breath. She'll burst," Naima thought in a panic. "Go ahead and cry. I won't tell. I promise," she whispered.

The choked sobs started again. After a few minutes Ruhama squeezed out some words. "I don't want to get married . . ." sob . . . "and go far away . . ." sob . . . "I don't know who my husband will be. He could be ugly and old and mean . . ." sob . . . "and I'll have to live in his father's house, and his mother will order me around . . ."

"But you have to get married. You're already fourteen years old."

"I know." Ruhama's sobs came faster.

"Don't cry." Naima patted her sister's shaking shoulders. "Ruhama never cries," she thought anxiously. "She's quiet as a dove. Mama always scolds me for squabbling with the boys and being prickly like a cactus pear instead of being sweet and helpful and quiet like Ruhama. Poor Ruhama. If she's crying, she must be really scared. I have to help her.

"What can you do to stop being worried or scared?" she wondered. "Papa and the boys pray to God. But Ruhama and I know only one prayer in the holy language, the prayer for lighting the Sabbath candles. So we would have to pray in Arabic. But God might not pay attention to Arabic prayers. Maybe we could ask the rabbi to talk to God for us. God would surely listen to the rabbi. Or maybe . . . ," and then she had an idea that was so good that she had to yank Ruhama's long braid to tell her.

"Ouch!" yelped Ruhama.

"Sssshhhh," Naima hissed. "I know what we can do. We'll ask Mama to take us to the shrine of Moussa ibn Dayyan. He'll help you for sure. Remember how he helped Samir the shoemaker to stop falling down and foaming at the mouth?"

Ruhama blew her nose and nodded. "That's where Mama went after you were born," she said. Her voice sounded a little less teary. "She had you and me—two girls—and Papa was very upset. So she asked Moussa ibn Dayyan to help her have a son. And nine months later she had Suleiman, and then Abraham, Moussa, Uzziah, and Menahem."

"What a powerful saint!" Naima gasped.

"But Mama won't take us," Ruhama said, and another sob hiccu͵ out. "She has too much work to do to get ready for the wedding. An͙ she's always tired because she's pregnant again."

"Then we'll go by ourselves!" Naima said boldly.

"By ourselves! But Moussa's shrine is far away—outside the Jewish quarter and outside the town wall. What if we don't get back in time and they lock the mellah gates? It's too dangerous."

Naima shivered. Being locked out of the mellah and being alone in the Muslim town after dark were too terrible to think about. "We won't be late," she said, trying to sound confident. "Moussa ibn Dayyan will take care of us."

Their chance came the very next day. Mama sent them to the big central market beyond the Jewish quarter to buy henna. The green henna leaves would be ground up and used to paint magical designs on Ruhama's and her mother's hands before the wedding. Two-year-old Menahem came with them, sucking his thumb as he bounced in a sling on Ruhama's back.

"Hurry." Naima tugged at Ruhama's belt as her sister bargained with the shopkeeper over the price of the henna. "We have to get back before the mellah gates close at sundown."

Ruhama tucked the henna leaves into her bag and proudly held up a coin. "We have a zolota left to spend. Come on!"

The girls hurried through the marketplace without stopping to look at the acrobats, the sword swallower, or the snake charmer. They ran on to the gateway of the city and pushed out through the crowds.

Beyond the gate a trail led up from the road. It zigzagged across the front of a round, bare hill, climbing higher and higher until it disappeared in a clump of dark-leaved trees at the top. Jews wearing humble black robes and straw sandals, by order of the sultan, and Muslims in bright, white and striped robes moved up and down the trail. At this hour, with afternoon shadows filling the wrinkles of the hillside, more pilgrims were going down than coming up.

Naima, who had been so daring the night before, itched with anxiety now. "Hurry," she kept saying as she tugged her sister along.

"Huwwwwy . . . huwwwwy . . ." Menahem imitated, swinging his fat, brown legs.

Ruhama, who had been miserable and frightened, bounced hopefully along the trail, chattering about everything they saw. "Do you know why

Muslims come to Moussa's shrine even though he's a Jewish holy man?''

"No . . . but hurry.''

"It's because he was a very good man, and his shrine is full of baraka. Mama said he came here many years ago from Safed with his little son. He came to collect money for the poor Jews of Safed, but he stayed to teach Torah. Then his son got sick and was about to die. Moussa begged God to take his life instead. And that's what God did. The boy got well, and Moussa died. He was buried up on this hill, and, ever since then, people come up here to ask Moussa to talk to God for them."

"Save your breath and walk faster," Naima said, with a wary eye on the sun.

Their straw sandals scuffed quickly over the dusty path. Far below, the heaped, white buildings of the city, its wall, and its tall, carved gate grew smaller and smaller. The trail turned once more, and suddenly they were in the deep shade of trees facing a small, square, whitewashed building with a domed roof. Two veiled women were just coming out of the arched doorway.

The girls left their slippers by the door and stepped into a dim, chilly room. In the center lay a long box covered with gleaming, blue and white tile—the tomb of Moussa ibn Dayyan.

Ruhama moved silently across to the tomb. Menahem looked around with wide, solemn eyes, and he sucked noisily on his thumb as Ruhama bent and kissed the cold edge of the tile. Then she rose and stood with her eyes closed and her hands pressed tightly together, taking deep breaths.

Menahem stopped sucking and fell asleep.

Naima waited. She took deep breaths too. She wanted to feel the blessed holiness, the baraka, but instead she felt uneasy. A low finger of light was already reaching through the doorway, and they had to get down the hill, through the town, and back to the mellah before sundown.

At last Ruhama turned away from the tomb, with her face shining and peaceful.

"She looks like my Ruhama again," Naima thought with relief. She squeezed her sister's hand happily and hurried her to the door. "Come on," she said. "We'll just make it."

But Naima's worries were not over. Outside the shrine a white-robed woman crouched on the ground beside their slippers. "Come here, little one," she said, looking up at Ruhama with huge black-rimmed eyes. "Sit beside me. I see that you face a great change. For only a zolota I will tell your fortune."

"Oh, no!" Naima yelped.

But Ruhama stopped. "Please, I have to know," she said, with her large, brown eyes pleading. She squatted before the woman and held out her hand. The woman looped a string of shells over Ruhama's palm, stared into it deeply, and then closed her eyes. For a moment she rocked back and forth, and then she muttered, "You are lucky. I see that a good thing will happen to you. A young man, a good man, will come. He will love you."

"W-will I love him too?" Ruhama asked shyly.

The woman opened her eyes. "That is not important," she said. "It is only important that he should love you." She took the coin from Ruhama's hand, tucked the shells under her robe, and settled back against the wall.

"A young man—a good man—for meeeee!" Ruhama laughed out loud as the girls went skidding down the winding trail—barefoot, clutching their straw slippers and the bag of henna. Menahem woke up and began kicking Ruhama's back, screaming with joy at the bouncing ride he was getting.

Through the city gate they ran with the shadows of the setting sun chasing them—through the great square, past the acrobats and the snake charmer, past the dark, tangy-smelling market booths where the merchants were lighting oil lamps.

Just ahead were the tall, metal mellah gates, already half-closed, with a crowd of black-robed Jews milling about in front of them.

"Move along," shouted Abdallah the gatekeeper. He prodded them through the narrow space with his stick. Wack . . . he struck at a boy who stood at the side instead of crowding forward with the others.

As the girls came running up, he swung his stick at them, catching Naima across the shoulders. "You're late. I shouldn't let you in, dhimmi pigs!" The sudden blow brought tears to Naima's eyes, but she rubbed them dry and pushed gratefully through the gate, behind her sister. It clanged shut behind her.

Ruhama didn't cry that night—at least Naima didn't hear her cry. The next few days and nights were so busy that there wasn't time for the girls to giggle together about their adventure. Aunts and uncles arrived from other towns; sleeping mats were rolled out in all the corners; cups of sweet peppermint tea and platters of pastries and fruit were served the entire day.

It was only on the first night of Ruhama's week-long wedding celebration that Naima had time to feel sad. She had watched her mother and all her aunts arrange Ruhama's hair and help Ruhama to dress. Now all the women of the wedding party were gathered in the courtyard wearing bright silk robes and sparkling jewelry. The men were celebrating at the bridegroom's house. Ruhama sat on a raised platform, leaning back against velvet pillows. Her hands were covered with rosy patterns made by the dye of the henna leaves. She wore heavy necklaces of gold chain, a glittering tiara in her thick, black, braided hair, and a heavy, shiny, brocade gown studded with pearls.

"She is as beautiful as a princess," Naima thought, "and she doesn't

look scared at all." Now it was Naima who wanted to cry. She wouldn't be able to whisper secrets to her sister at night, or to laugh with her while they sorted grain or washed clothes. It would be so lonely in that house full of boys.

"Sssssst," Ruhama hissed, waving a jeweled finger. Her eyes danced with excitement. "Come closer. I have something to tell you."

Naima leaned close.

"Moussa ibn Dayyan did it!"

"Did what?" asked Naima.

"He got me a handsome, young bridegroom. Yesterday Mama called me to the window and showed him to me. He was walking home from the synagogue with his father—and he's tall and has curly hair and a sweet smile. I'm so happy I can hardly sit still."

"I—I'm ha-happy tooooooo." Naima tried to smile, but, instead, before she knew it, she was sniffling and sobbing, and tears were pouring down her face. "Oh, I'll miss you, Ruhama," she wailed. "I wish we had another sister." She covered her face with her hands and turned away. It would be awful if she smeared Ruhama's beautiful, hennaed hands with tears.

Ruhama began to giggle in a little-girl way, as if she weren't a bride at all, and pulled Naima closer. She pointed across the room to where her mother sat on a pillow with the other women, resting a teacup on her bulging belly. "Maybe you'll have a sister very soon." She whispered into Naima's ear, "I talked to Moussa ibn Dayyan about that too, after I finished asking for his help with my marriage."

"Oh!" Naima clapped both hands to her mouth. "If Papa only knew!" She burst into delighted laughter, and Ruhama joined in, laughing so hard that all her earrings, bracelets, and necklaces began to jingle.

"Ah—ah-ah-aaaaah . . ." the crowd of women began to sway and call out a wailing celebration cry. The musicians had arrived. It was time to hold up and admire the wedding gifts. Then there would be music and dancing and lots of good food.

Naima rubbed her face dry and skipped back to sit with the other girls. Tonight she would sing and dance until the musicians were too tired to go on. She and Ruhama had so much to celebrate.

CHAPTER

14

Sarah rubbed the next coin until it began to gleam. "I think it's silver, and it's so pretty," she said. "There's a picture of a city on it."

"Good, that will make it easier to look up," said Jamie. "Number Fifteen will also be easy to find because it's so big. So we're getting to be experts at looking up coins. But what good will it do us? We're not discovering anything about Uncle Otto."

"It doesn't hurt to learn a little history," said Grandma, "and I still have hope." She hunted through the coin book for Number Fourteen.

GOLD DUCAT, 1796
Minted in Regensburg, Germany. On one side it shows the city of Regensburg with a bridge over the river. On the other side is a portrait of the German emperor.

"This coin was used during a hectic time," said Grandma. "People were fighting for freedom in Germany and all over Europe during the early 1800s. When the revolution in Germany was crushed, many German Jews and non-Jews came to the United States. Until that time, most of the Jews in the United States were Sephardim, which means that their ancestors had come from Spain. The German Jews were called Ashkenazim, and they brought different customs. It took many years for the two kinds of Jews to be comfortable with each other.

The Egg and Potato Passover

Pennsylvania, 1850

They were only three hours out of Wilkes-Barre, Pennsylvania, when the snow started. At first there were just a few light flakes—just enough to melt in nine-year-old Isaac Heller's eyelashes. But Isaac's father watched the thickening sky anxiously. He flicked the switch over the bony rear of Shlimazel the horse and muttered, "Move!"

Shlimazel clip-clopped faster, and the peddler's wagon creaked and lurched in and out of ruts. But the flakes fell faster too, filling the ruts, smoothing the rocks and hollows, and soon hiding the road behind a curtain of frozen fluff.

"This cursed country!" Isaac's father exploded. "It's spring, the eve of Passover. How can there be a snowstorm?"

"It's not cursed. It's a wonderful country—much better than Germany. You told me that yourself," Isaac pointed out, always ready for an argument.

His father wasn't listening. He was leaning forward, trying to see. The snow already covered his broad-brimmed hat and crusted his thick eyebrows and mustache. "We can't go on. We can't see the road," he said. "If we fall into a ditch and break an axle . . ."

"Th-then we'll freeze," Isaac finished the thought and gulped a mouthful of snowflakes. He pulled the tattered bearskin cover up to his chin and stared around desperately, trying to see through the flakes that were already turning blue in the twilight.

"Papa, Papa!" He jumped up from the seat. "Over there—something. I think it's a house!"

"Baruch Hashem," Mister Heller murmured gratefully. The dim, gray shape with a faint square of yellow-lit window had to be a house.

He looped the wagon reins back, and they jumped to the ground and struggled up toward the lighted window. A low-roofed, wooden building appeared out of the snow.

Isaac's father knocked at the door, and a woman in a wide apron with her hair pulled tightly back into a bun opened it. A boy, as tall as Isaac, wearing knickers, stood beside her.

"Please, Missus, vee have our vay lost in the snow," said Mister Heller in his German-accented English. "Could you give us shelter?"

"Furriners!" snorted the woman. "We don't allow furriners here." She tried to close the door, but Isaac's father quickly placed his snowy boot in the way. "Please," he said again.

"John," cried the woman.

A thin, sandy-haired man came to the door. He looked from Mister Heller to Isaac, almost hidden behind his father, and then at the silently falling snow. "Mother, we can't turn these people away," he said gently. "The Good Book says, 'Thou shalt neither vex a stranger nor oppress him, for you were strangers in the land of Egypt.' "

"But I won't sleep a wink all night with furriners in the house," she protested.

"Then they'll bed down in the barn." The man quickly pulled on boots, a cap, and a jacket. Holding a lantern high in the thick swirl of flakes, he went down to the road with them and led patient Shlimazel and the wagon back up to the dark barn behind the farmhouse.

"There's oats and water here for your horse," said the farmer, "and up the ladder is the hay loft." He led them past a pen where Isaac dimly saw a great sow and a cluster of piglets, then past a stall housing a horse, and past another stall with two large, quiet cows. Isaac wanted to hold his nose at the strange barn smells, but he didn't dare.

They climbed the ladder to the loft. "The hay is itchy," the farmer said, "but it'll be warm enough. Bossie, Elmer, and Bonnie give off a lot of heat. I'll leave you the lantern. Just be sure to blow it out before you go to sleep."

"A thanks to you. God bless you," said Isaac's father as the farmer climbed back down. When Mister Heller turned back to Isaac, he found tears running down the boy's face.

"What's wrong?"

"It's the first night of Passover, and we're in a strange place where they don't want us, with just Bossie and Bonnie and Elmer," Isaac sniffled. "And I'm cold and it smells bad, and there are no matzos, kugel, and tzimmes and . . . Papa, I'm sorry." He swallowed his tears and wiped his face with his sleeve. "I didn't mean to cry. It just came. I wanted so much to be in Wilkes-Barre with Aunt Hannah and Uncle Velvl for Passover."

"My son, wherever we are, God is with us. And tonight even the prophet Elijah will join us because he comes to every seder, even to a barn in Pennsylvania. First I'll climb down to brush and feed Shlimazel, and then we'll wash up in the snow and prepare our seder."

*   *   *

A clean shirt was spread over a table of heaped hay. In the center sat a pewter dish that held four cold, boiled potatoes and three hard-boiled eggs. Two pewter cups of water and Mister Heller's tiny traveler's candlesticks were set securely on one of the beams of the barn. The candles made flickering shadows against the peaked roof. Isaac and his father, red-faced from the snow-wash, leaned back against the straw, wearing their black yarmulkes, and began the seder.

"Baruch Atah Adonai Elohenu Melech ha'olam," Mister Heller began, singing the blessing over the wine, holding high one cup of water. Suddenly they heard footsteps on the ladder. A moment later, the farmer's boy poked his head above the loft floor. His eyes, racing from the yarmulkes to the dish to the candles, opened wide.

He gulped, took a deep breath, and said in a rush, "Here's some soup and bread for you. My mom said to tell you she's sorry she was so unchristian before." He held out a steaming pot and a handkerchief-wrapped bundle.

"A thanks to your mama," Isaac's father answered gravely, "but vee are Israelites and tonight is the first night of Passover, so this food vee may not eat."

"A thanks," Isaac blurted too. The smell of the soup was making his mouth water.

"Israelites?" The boy's eyes seemed about to pop out. "Like in the Bible? Were you singing in Hebrew?"

"Vee vere telling the story of Passover in Hebrew," Mister Heller answered.

"Gosh," the boy gasped. "Gosh!" His head disappeared, and they heard him scramble down the ladder and race to the barn door.

"Now will they make us leave?" Isaac asked anxiously.

"This is America, not Germany," answered his father. But his hand trembled as he raised a potato and began to recite the words, "Ha lachma anya . . . , this is the bread of affliction which our ancestors ate in the land of Egypt." Then he continued, "Let all who are in need come and celebrate Passover with us." Putting down the potato, he said to Isaac, "Are you ready to ask the Four Questions, my son?"

"Mah nishtanah halayelah hazeh mikol haleylot," Isaac began to sing. He knew the words by heart because he had practiced them for days as the peddler wagon rolled along, stopping at farms and villages where his father sold cloth, needles, pots, hammers, and a thousand other things. But he had never expected to ask the questions in a dark, lonely barn.

"Shebechol haleylot anu ochlin chametz umatzah," he sang on.

Wood scraped on wood as the barn door was opened.

Isaac kept singing as footsteps creaked along the floor below. "If they make us leave, what will we do," he thought fearfully, even as his lips moved. The tears started to come again, but he squeezed them back and sang through to the final words. Then he slowly turned, looking toward the ladder.

Two pairs of wide eyes were watching him—the farmer's and the boy's. The farmer cleared his throat uneasily. "We don't want to interrupt you," he said. "We just kinda wondered if we could listen. We're Baptists, but we know about the feast of Passover from the Good Book. We've never seen an Israelite before, and we wondered . . ."

Isaac's father breathed a deep sigh of relief. "Vee vould be honored." He stretched out a welcoming hand. "Please, please climb up. Isaac, pile up the straw so our guests should lean back."

The candles burned down and died, but the lantern flickered as Isaac's father sang, repeating as much of the Passover Haggadah as he could remember. When it was time for the seder meal, he divided the potatoes and the eggs into four portions, and the farmer, his son, and the "Israelites" ate together. And, at the very end, Isaac and his father sang "To the next year in Jerusalem" and "Chad Gadya" in loud, happy voices.

Then the barn was silent again, except for quiet crunching as one of the cows worked on a last wisp of hay. The farmer chuckled, slapped his knee, and said, "I wonder what Bossie, Elmer, and Bonnie made of that." He turned to Mister Heller. "My missus feels bad that she was unfriendly, and she asked if you and the boy would come over and visit when your feast was done."

Down the ladder they climbed. They went past the restless horse, the chewing cows, and the squirming piglets with their huge, peaceful mother. "That's funny," Isaac thought. "They don't smell so bad anymore." At the house the farmer's wife greeted them with a stiff smile and led them to the kitchen table where a large platter was piled high with more boiled potatoes and eggs.

"It's a wonder you Israelites keep your strength up with just eggs and potatoes," she marveled. "When you're done eating, I hope you'll sing some hymns with us. We Baptists are great ones for singing."

"And vee Israelites love on Passover to sing," Isaac's father said. Isaac nodded in agreement with a mouth full of potato.

Afterwards they gathered by the warm stove. The farmer strummed on a banjo and led them all in hymns from the Hebrew Scriptures. Then the farmer's boy taught them "Pop Goes the Weasel" and "Clementine." Soon they were stamping and laughing and clapping together.

At the end of a wailing chorus of "you are lost and gone forever, oh, my darlin' Clementine," the boy whispered to Isaac, "Can I see your horns?"

"My what?"

"Your horns," the boy said as he tapped the top of Isaac's head. "All Israelites have horns."

"My horns?" Isaac clapped his hands to his head and felt around.

"No, son," said the farmer, "the Bible tells us that Moses had horns. Maybe regular Israelites don't have them."

Now Isaac's father was puzzled. "Moses had horns?"

"Sure, it says so right here." The farmer jumped up to fetch his worn Bible, and the adults leaned over it eagerly, discussing the English word "horns." Isaac's father explained that it must be a translation of the Hebrew word "karnayim" which had two meanings: horns and rays. "I think that rays of light from Moses's head came, not horns," he said politely.

"Well now, I'm not so sure." The farmer shook his head and continued the discussion.

But the boy turned to Isaac and whispered, "I don't care about all that, do you?"

Isaac shook his head.

"Good! I'll show you my collection."

The boy lifted a canvas bag from a hook and spilled out four Indian arrowheads, the delicate skull of a fox, a lump of gleaming fool's gold, and two coins: a continental penny and a small British coin. "My grandfather gave me the coins," he said. "They're real old, and they're from far away."

"I have here also some coins," said Isaac. He emptied his pockets, and they settled down to compare and play.

The coals in the stove had cooled to dull red when Isaac and his father finally started back to the barn. The snowfall had ended, but snow was piled in gentle ripples and billows around the fences and outbuildings of the farm.

"Good night," the farmer's wife called after them. "I'll have some more potatoes and eggs ready for you in the morning."

"Ugh," Isaac groaned to himself.

"A thanks," his father called back, "and vat I can pay you for your hospitality?"

"Not a copper penny," she cried. "You're our guests."

*   *   *

"It was a strange seder night," said Isaac's father as he settled back into the crackling straw. "Your Aunt Hannah and Uncle Velvl will never believe us."

"It was the best seder I ever had," Isaac said happily. "Papa, may I give the boy my gold ducat for his collection? He likes things from far away."

"You may. And, since our hostess won't let us pay her, I'll find some pretty cloth in the wagon so that she can make a new dress for herself."

Isaac burrowed deeper into the straw and curled his legs up. "Eggs and potatoes for breakfast," he thought sleepily. "Ugh!"

CHAPTER
15

SILVER PIASTER, 1880
Coined in Constantinople, Turkey. It is inscribed with the name of the sultan and the year in which he came to power.

"Back to Turkey again," Jamie said.

"The coin is Turkish," Grandma said," but it could have come from Syria or Palestine or any of the other countries of that area. Turkey ruled them all. This coin might even have been used by the chalutzim, the Jewish pioneers, who came to build a homeland in Palestine in the late 1800s and the early 1900s.

"Maybe one of the pioneers was named Otto Schwartz," suggested Sarah hopefully.

"No," Grandma laughed. "I don't think Uncle Otto ever went to Palestine. But one of his best friends went. Remember, I told you there were three best friends who grew up together in Hashvata. Their names were Shmulik, Srulik, and Itzik. Shmulik came to America and became my father, Sam. Itzik moved to Prague and changed his name to Otto. And Srulik was the one who went to Palestine."

"Talk to me, little piaster," Sarah said, half-laughing and half-pleading as she stared at the coin. "Tell me if you were ever in Srulik's pocket."

Shmulik, Srulik, and Itzik

Russia, 1900

"So you're playing with buttons on the bench instead of reading the Bible," snapped Reb Sender, the cheder teacher. "Come over here, Shmulik. Bend over. You're going to get a thrashing you'll never forget!"

Stubby, dark-haired, little Shmulik bit his lip and climbed over the bench to go to the teacher.

"Me too, Reb Sender." Freckled Srulik jumped up. "I was playing with buttons too."

"And me too," cried blue-eyed Itzik with the blond curls.

Reb Sender scowled at the three boys and felt his arm growing tired even before he started the thrashing. "Three good-for-nothings. You'll all come to a bad end, God forbid," he yelled, shaking his bony forefinger at them. "Give me those buttons. I'll let you go this time. But God help you if I catch you again playing during a lesson."

That's how it was with Shmulik, Srulik, and Itzik. They always stuck together.

When they finished studying the Bible in Reb Sender's tumbledown, little cheder, they went on to the yeshivah together and studied from the huge books of the Talmud and the commentaries. They shared their lunches and their Chanukah gelt. At Purimtime they clowned through the streets together wearing their sisters' dresses, and at Simchat Torah they danced happily with the Torahs, one behind the other, in the small, wooden synagogue of their mostly Jewish town of Hashvata in Russia.

If the pogrom hadn't happened in the spring, after they became bar mitzvah, they might have married and settled down in straw-roofed houses, side by side, and raised children.

But one afternoon, right before Passover, Mottel the wagon driver came clattering into town, cracking his whip. His horse reared to a stop in the marketplace as Mottel yelled, "Jews, go home and close your shutters. Pogromchiks are coming!"

Pogroms were nothing new to Hashvata. Every few years the Russian peasants who lived around the town got angry at their Jewish neighbors. Sometimes a peasant decided he had been cheated by a Jewish merchant; sometimes he claimed he had been robbed by the Jew who collected taxes for the lord of the district; and sometimes, especially after a fiery Easter sermon in church, the peasants decided to punish the Jews for killing their savior. Then they grabbed sticks, hoes, and axes and came charging into town to break windows, beat people, and drag off silverware, clothing, and furniture.

Jews were often hurt, even killed, in these attacks. So when they heard the cry "pogrom," they gathered their children, raced home, nailed shut the doors and windows, and huddled in the dark, praying for God's help.

Shmulik, Srulik, and Itzik, like everyone else, had been terrified during the last pogrom. When they met in the marketplace afterwards, Shmulik burst out furiously, "Next time I won't hide! I'll fight them!"

"We can't fight. There aren't enough of us," Srulik said. "First they'd kill us, and then they'd destroy the town."

Itzik leaned on a barrel and chewed his lip thoughtfully. Then he said,

"There's another way. We'll trick them. It's the only thing we can do."
And he told them his plan.

* * *

On the spring day when Mottel yelled, "Pogromchiks are coming," the
boys were studying at the long, wooden table in the yeshivah. The teachers
hurried to close the shutters. After the other boys ran home, Shmulik,
Srulik, and Itzik went in the opposite direction. They ran through the
alleys to the edge of town. Then they ducked behind the hedgerows in
the fields and crept toward the nearest farmhouse. It belonged to Ivan
the potter, the worst of the Jew-haters.

From the road beyond the field they heard the rattle of empty carts
being driven toward town. Excited, hoarse voices cried, "Christ-killers
. . . thieves . . . Jewish cheats . . . we'll fill the carts with their gold
and silver . . . it's all stolen anyhow . . . the bloodsuckers . . . teach
them a lesson. . . ."

The boys clenched their fists and crouched low. When the sounds moved
past them, they ran on. They reached the yard of the whitewashed farmhouse just as screams began to rise from Hashvata—screams, then the
crash of falling glass and the thump of sticks and axes on doors and shutters.

"We have to hurry," Itzik gasped. "Srulik, see if anybody is inside.
Shmulik, tie a stack of straw together for a torch." Itzik himself ran around
the yard flapping his arms to shoo the chickens, pigs, and goats out into
the field.

Srulik dashed out. "Nobody is inside. But they left a big pot cooking
on the fire. That's good. They'll think it was an accident."

Itzik ducked through the low doorway of the farmhouse, holding the
bundle of straw. He poked it into the cooking fire. Then he touched the
burning straw to the heaped feather quilt on the bed in the corner, to
the straw covering the floor, and to the baskets on the shelf. Wisps of
smoke rose from the damp floor, and tiny flames began to bite into the
edges of the quilt.

From the doorway Srulik gasped at the creeping flames. "Wait," he
cried, "maybe we shouldn't . . . how can we burn somebody's house?"
He wanted to run in and stamp out the flames, but Itzik grabbed his
arm. "Come on," Itzik yelled, pulling Srulik out to the yard. "We have
to do it, Srulik. We have no choice."

With a great "whoosh" the straw on the floor caught and filled the
room with fire.

Back to the field they raced, tumbled over the hedgerow, and fell behind it. Black smoke began to pour from the windows of the farmhouse. They could still hear faraway cries and screams from Hashvata.

"Turn around, you murdering pogromchiks. Look back and see the fire," Srulik muttered through clenched teeth. "Stop hitting and smashing!"

Flames darted around the eaves of the house and licked at the roof. Black smoke billowed up into the air. Then, as though they had heard Srulik's words, the peasants turned and saw the smoke. The deep Russian voices grew louder; the sounds of smashing and thumping died out.

"They saw it. They're coming. Let's get out of here," Shmulik whispered.

Bent low, the boys crept back the way they had come. Halfway to town they again heard the pounding of feet and the grinding of cartwheels.

Voices called, "It's Petya's house . . . no, it's Ivan's." "My milk goat, save my milk goat!" a woman cried, "and the suckling pigs! Oh, hurry."

The urgent voices moved on. And Shmulik, Srulik, and Itzik crept along behind the hedgerow until they reached town.

"We did it! We saved the town!" They hugged and clapped each other on the back and then fell, laughing and panting for breath, against the wooden fence of the synagogue.

Old Moisheh the synagogue caretaker peered fearfully over the fence. "Thank God, it's you," he whispered when he recognized the boys. "Did you hear what happened? It was God's miracle. A sudden fire. All the pogromchiks ran home."

"We heard, Reb Moisheh," the boys answered, nodding and smiling. But, when they turned to each other, the laughter was gone. Just as they shared everything, now they shared a strange sadness and tiredness.

"So this time we helped God to save the town. What will happen next time?" Shmulik asked softly.

Srulik shook his head. "For me there won't be a next time. I'll never burn anyone's house again. But I won't sit here and wait for another pogrom. I'll go to Palestine. In my own land nobody will be able to push me around."

"My father says there's nothing in Palestine but malaria mosquitoes and camels. You'll starve," Shmulik argued. "When I leave Hashvata, I'll go to America where my big brother lives. He wrote us that it's a golden land."

"I won't stay here either," Itzik said. "My uncle has a big store in Prague. He asked my father to let me come and help him. Until today I didn't want to go, but this pogrom changed my mind. I'll go to Prague, and I'll work hard. Someday I'll be rich and powerful—so rich and powerful that no pogromchik will dare raise a fist at me. You'll see."

Srulik looked down at the ground to hide his tears. "I thought we'd always be together," he said softly.

"We'll always write to each other," Itzik said.

"We'll never stop being friends," Shmulik added.

"Never, never," they said, clasping each other's hands tightly.

*   *   *

Before the boys turned fourteen, and before the next pogrom hit Hashvata, Shmulik, Srulik, and Itzik sadly said goodbye to each other. They and their families left Hashvata and went in different directions.

Srulik became Yisrael, a farmer in Palestine. He sent a letter containing a Turkish coin to each of his friends. "You see, there's more here than mosquitoes and camels," he wrote. "There's also a Turkish government. Someday it will be a Jewish government."

Shmulik became Sam, a dress manufacturer in New York. "The streets aren't exactly paved with gold, but this is a free and wonderful country," he wrote.

And Itzik became Otto, owner of a department store in Prague. "I wish you were both here with me," he wrote. "There's no better land in the whole world than Czechoslovakia. Srulik, many thanks for your Turkish coin. I'll add it to my synagogue's coin collection."

CHAPTER
16

One small, brown coin sat alone under the kitchen light.

"There sits our last chance," said Jamie. "It looks like a penny, but it's probably more useless than a penny. It won't give us a clue, and it won't buy even a piece of bubble gum. Come on, Grandma, let's face it. Old Uncle Otto didn't want to tell his secret. He took it down into his grave with him."

"Jamie, you are absolutely wrong!" cried Grandma. "Toward the end he was desperately trying to tell us, but he was too sick. That's why we have to keep trying." She pushed up her glasses and read the writing on the coin. "It says 'Palestine' in English and in Hebrew, and there's Arabic writing on it that probably says 'Palestine' too."

"Palestine," Sarah repeated, and her fingers went scrambling through the book.

BRONZE ONE MIL, 1938
Coined in Palestine by the government of the British Mandate. On one side it has an olive branch with the inscription "One Mil" in English, Hebrew, and Arabic. On the other side is the word "Palestine" in the three languages with the date.

"The British ruled Palestine from the end of the First World War until 1948 when the State of Israel was founded," said Grandma. "They were supposed to help the Jews build a homeland, but during a good part of that time they tried to prevent Jews from getting into the country."

"So the British were ruling Palestine when Uncle Otto's daughter got there. Right?" asked Sarah.

"Right," said Grandma.

"Could that be a clue?"

"If that's a clue, I'm a cheese blintz with strawberry jam," Jamie yelped.

"You must be getting hungry, Jamie," Grandma said. "Finish drawing the coin while I start frying the blintzes. I told your mother I invited you two for supper tonight. While we eat, we'll decide what to do next. We're not licked yet!"

Honor Your Father

Palestine, 1938

Late one night in the summer of 1938, a rusty truck rattled along the cobblestone streets of a French fishing village. Under the soggy canvas in the back, twenty boys and girls sat bobbing and shaking, their teeth chattering with the truck's movement.

"I-I f-feel like an eggnog," stuttered Lisa. She was a small girl with a mop of curly, blond hair—so small that she might have bounced out if she hadn't been wedged between her friends Hayyim and Hildy.

"An eggnog," skinny Hayyim groaned, clutching his stomach. "I'd love an eggnog right now. I'm starving!"

"You're always starving. You're a human garbage can," said Hildy unsympathetically. "Don't worry. There will be food on the ship."

"Who cares about food? I'm too excited to eat," Lisa said. "We're nearly out of Europe. I wish I could tell my father. He was so frightened. He was sure we'd be arrested or shot on the way. But he was wrong. In a little while we'll be on a ship on our way to Palestine."

"Hurray for Palestine!" Hayyim cheered. "Everybody up! Let's dance a hora." He struggled to his feet, but, as the truck lurched, he fell, sprawling across Lisa's lap.

"Sssshhh!" Levi the Palestinian hissed a warning from the front seat. "No noise. We'll have the French police on our heads."

"He's so cute," Hildy whispered, nodding toward Levi. Lisa nodded, starry-eyed.

"Sssshhhh!"

They hushed. Levi was handsome, in a big-nosed, broad-shouldered way, and they were both a little bit in love with him. But he was also their leader, and his word was law. He had been sent to Europe by the Mossad, an organization of Palestinian Jews, and he was risking his life to help them escape from the Nazis and to bring them to Palestine. Lisa settled back against the side of the truck and thought about the first time she saw Levi.

* * *

It was an afternoon in early spring when Levi came to the meeting of Lisa's Zionist club in Prague. He was tall and sunburned and spoke to the group of boys and girls in a deep, earnest voice.

"I've been sent to you by the Jews of Palestine," he told them.

"Are you a real Palestinian, a pioneer?" Lisa asked, awestruck.

"A real one," he laughed. "Here's proof." And he flipped a small coin into her lap. "See, it says 'Palestine' in three languages." Then his face became serious again. "Some of you know me already. You know that tomorrow I will lead you out of Czechoslovakia on a secret route to Palestine."

Plump, rosy Hildy, sitting beside Lisa, nodded soberly. Her suitcase was packed.

"This may be the last group I'll be able to take. The British are trying to stop us. I have room for one more person."

"Oh, Lisa, come with us," Hildy pleaded.

Lisa shook her head. "I can't leave my father. He's all alone except for me. I'll come someday."

Levi's voice was sad as he said, "Someday may be too late."

On the way home from the meeting Lisa tried to shake off the memory of the grim words, "Someday may be too late." She was full of news to tell her father about Hildy's going to Palestine and about Levi. And she had a new coin to give him for his precious collection. But, when her father came in the door, she forgot everything. Otto Schwartz's stiff homburg hat was dusty and dented and pulled down over a bruise on his forehead. His proud, straight back was bent. When she reached up to hug him, he held her at a distance, as though he were afraid her hug would make him break down.

"I have a hard thing to tell you," he said, "and I must say it quickly. A gang of Nazis broke the windows of the store today and smeared 'Jude' on the walls. When I tried to stop them, they beat me, and my good friend, the police captain, refused to arrest them. He is afraid of them. . . ."

"Poor Papa, what will you do?"

He went on in a harsh, tight voice, forcing out each word, "Nothing. I can only wait for this craziness to end. But you must go away. It's too dangerous for you here, Lisa. I want you to be in a safe place until we can teach these Nazi hooligans a lesson. I've made arrangements to send you to England until things quiet down."

"You're sending me away?" Lisa pulled free of his hard grip. She straightened up to her full five-foot height, with her blue eyes blazing and her pointy chin firm. "Do you think I'm a package that you can send? I'm sixteen years old. I can make up my own mind!"

"You're a child. I know what's best for you. You'll do as you're told."

"No," she said. "If I have to leave you and leave home, I want to go with my friends. I want to go to Palestine."

"That's dangerous, and it's against the law," her father shouted. His face was grayish white around the purple bruise, and his pale, blue eyes were frightened. "You're a soft, pampered, little girl. If you go with those crazy Zionists, you'll be sneaking across borders and hiding in the woods, and in the end they'll catch you and throw you in jail—or shoot you."

He took a sobbing breath. "You're all I have. I'm afraid for you." Then, ashamed of his weakness, he straightened up and shouted, "I forbid you to think of going to Palestine!"

"You can't forbid me!" she shouted back.

Her father raised his hand angrily, stopped himself, and asked hoarsely, "Have you forgotten the commandment, 'Honor your father and your mother' ?"

Lisa didn't answer. He turned away and walked slowly out of the room.

She lay awake that night, crying and arguing with herself. "He *wants* to send me away; it's not as if I'm leaving him . . . he can't order me around . . . I won't go to London . . . I belong here or in Palestine." She fell asleep as the sky was turning gray with dawn. Her mind was made up.

When Lisa came down later that morning, her father had already left for the store. Her carfare and lunch money for school lay on the table. She placed her goodbye note and the coin from Palestine beside them.

"Goodbye, house; goodbye, Papa," she whispered, looking around through a blur of tears. "Goodbye, Mama," she kissed the yellowing picture of her long-gone mother, which stood on the bookcase. Then she pulled on her hiking boots, grabbed her backpack, and ran to join her friends at the train station.

* * *

Abruptly Lisa was shaken out of her memories and dropped back into the present, into the crowded truck with Levi, Hildy, and the others. The truck had swung in a wide circle that slid everybody to one side in a squealing, giggling pile. With a screech of brakes it stopped short.

Levi's voice called softly, "Everybody out. Fast!"

They scrambled down, got a quick glimpse of a puddle-filled wharf, felt a warm drizzle, and smelled fish. Then they were hustled onto a long pier over dark, lapping water and into a boat that bobbed at the end.

"Sit close together," Levi called. "There are more coming."

"More?" Groans rose up.

"This must be a sardine boat, and we're the sardines," Hayyim wise-cracked.

"Oh, no," Hildy sighed, "you're thinking of food again."

More feet drummed along the pier. Another group of young people hurried aboard. There were yelps as knees and elbows jabbed and people bumped each other. Before they had settled down, the engine began to throb beneath them, and the boat moved slowly out to sea.

The next few days on "Sardine Heaven," Hayyim's name for their little ship, were crowded but happy. There was no room to dance horas, but they could sing and talk without being shushed. Sometimes Levi came to sit with Lisa and Hildy and told them about his kibbutz and about the orange trees and the bright sun of the Land of Israel. "I was right to come," Lisa thought, bubbling with joy. But, when she thought of her father, she felt guilty.

At night, with her head against Hildy's shoulder, she looked up at the stars and wrote endless letters in her head. "Dear Papa, so much has happened since I left you. I got thinner and a little taller, I think. And my hair is awful. But I'm so happy. We're going to build a Jewish homeland in Palestine—me, Hildy, Levi, and Hayyim. And you can come and open a store in Tel Aviv, and we'll be together again. I can't wait till you meet Levi. You'll like him. Hildy and I both want to marry him. . . ." The letter turned into a rosy dream as Lisa fell asleep.

On the last evening Levi climbed to the top of a pile of crates and shouted, "Chaverim, we will reach the coast of Palestine tonight."

People hugged and jumped up and down and began to sing, "Kol od balevav . . . ," the words of the Zionist anthem, "Hatikvah."

Levi sang too, and, as they finished, he raised his arms for silence. "We've come through great dangers together," he said. "Now we are nearly home, but we have one more danger to face."

The boys and girls on deck exchanged quick, anxious looks. Hildy and Lisa pressed close to each other.

"There are British ships patrolling the coast of Palestine. They will try to stop us from landing. They call us illegal immigrants, and, if they catch us, they'll send us back to Europe."

"We won't go!" Hayyim shouted. There were more angry shouts. Some people started to cry.

Again the long arms were raised. "We'll make it, in spite of them."

Levi's voice was calm. "From now on, no singing, no loud voices. Put every important thing, money, or identification in your pockets. You may not be able to take your suitcases or backpacks. Then lie back and sleep. In a few hours we'll need all our strength."

Slowly the sky turned blue-black, then black. The stars were so large and close Lisa felt she could touch them. Hildy fell asleep with her head in Lisa's lap and the pale tracks of tears on her cheeks. The only sounds were the throb of the engines and the ripple of waves slipping past the bow. The thump of her heart seemed to Lisa to be the loudest sound of all. "I'm scared," she thought. "I didn't think I'd ever have to be scared again."

A faraway, booming sound began to grow louder.

Hayyim stirred beside Lisa. "It's the surf," he whispered. "We must be near Palestine."

"Palestine . . . Palestine . . ." the words raced around the boat like an electric current. Hildy woke, shivering, with her teeth chattering. Lisa squeezed her friend's icy hands and took off her own jacket for Hildy to wear.

From the wheelhouse above, a light blinked across the water. Within seconds a light answered from shore. The boat changed course slightly and headed toward the light. "We're going in. We're safe!" Hayyim whispered happily.

Suddenly a weird, rising and falling wail cut through the stillness. A siren. Far to the west a dark shape was blocking out the stars. A long finger of light poked from it, picked its way along the smooth sea, and found the small boat. Everybody fell flat, blinded by the sudden brightness. A moment later a voice sounded across the water, "This is the captain of His Majesty's Ship Falcon. You are in restricted waters. Drop anchor and identify yourself."

The engine of the small boat began to throb harder. The boat trembled as it rushed faster and faster, directly toward the lights blinking on shore.

Hildy was sobbing. Lisa held her tight and tried to hear Levi's voice above the pounding of the engines. "Stay calm. When the ship hits bottom, go over the side and walk or swim to shore. Our people will be waiting in the water to help you. Help is waiting."

"I can't swim!" Hildy cried. Lisa was shaking too. "It'll be all right, Hildy. They'll help us."

A line of white sand shone out of the darkness ahead. The boat roared toward it until, with a sudden, rasping screech, it tore into the seabed

and reared up on its bow. Lisa and Hildy slid forward along the deck in the screaming, struggling mass of other passengers. Then the boat shuddered backward with a terrible, crunching, groaning noise and began to tip slowly onto its side.

"Come on!" Lisa cried, dragging Hildy with her. "Take a breath!" They fell over the side, hit the water, and sank. Lisa lost Hildy's hand as she struggled to push upward. Lisa's head broke through the surface. She took a great gulp of air. In the darkness voices were calling out in Hebrew. Then she was sinking again—turning and turning and sinking. Her lungs were bursting, her eyes popping. "Papa, Papa," she was crying inside her head, "I'm drowning!"

With a sudden jerk her head broke the surface again. Somebody was pulling her hair. She sputtered and gasped, struggling to get loose. The grip was too strong. Now they had her arms. Her eyes stung as she tried to see.

Men and women, boys and girls, strangers were standing in the black water in a long line that led from the sinking boat, through the breakers, to the white, sand shore. They were Levi's people, Palestinian Jews. Hands were pushing her through the water, from person to person. She tried to say, "Find Hildy . . . she can't swim!" But no sound came out except wheezing gasps as she was carried along until she felt sand beneath her feet. Then she stumbled through the surf and fell onto the sand.

"No time to rest yet." Strong arms shoved her toward a truck.

"No!" She pulled away and stumbled back to the surf calling, "Hildy!"

At the water's edge two dark figures were working over a still body. Lisa recognized her water-soaked jacket, and then she saw Hildy's pale, still face.

"Let's go! The British patrols are coming." She was pulled away and lifted into the back of a truck. She fell against the other boys and girls, all of them cold and wet and salty as herrings, as Hayyim would've said.

"Hildy, Hildy," she sobbed. "Oh, Papa, I'm all alone."

"No, you're not alone," said a gentle but unfamiliar voice. "You're home." Warm arms held her close and rocked her with the rocking of the truck.

*   *   *

Weeks later, when Lisa was well again, she wrote a letter to her father. She told him about the ship and the rescue and about Hildy, the friend she had lost. "Please come to Palestine, Papa," she wrote. "I miss you very much." Then she sealed the envelope and mailed it to Mr. Otto Schwartz, 319 Rosselgasse, Prague, Czechoslovakia.

The reply came two months later. It was her own envelope, unopened, and on it the Czechoslovak postal service had stamped, "Unknown at this address."

"Next to chocolate chip cookies, cheese blintzes are my favorite," Jamie said and stuffed a huge blintz into his mouth.

"How can you eat? Why aren't you miserable like me?" Sarah protested. "We're all finished with the coins, and we have gotten absolutely nowhere!"

"Not exactly nowhere," said Grandma, trying very hard to sound cheerful. "We discovered that the coins follow more than 3,000 years of Jewish history, all the way from the time of Moses until the time just before the Second World War."

"So what good does that do us?"

"I don't know yet. I'm thinking," Grandma said. She slowly spread strawberry jam on her blintz and dotted it with little dabs of sour cream while she waited for inspiration.

"Palestine," Jamie mumbled with his mouth full. "Didn't Palestine become Israel?"

"Yes, it did. In 1948. Chew and swallow. Then you can talk some more."

Jamie swallowed. "And you said that Palestine is where Uncle Otto's daughter went."

Grandma and Sarah nodded.

"Maybe she's still there. If we could find her, she might know something. How could we find her?"

"I know how!" Sarah cried. "We can do what Grandma did for her garage sale. Put an ad in the newspaper!"

"Do they have newspapers in Israel?" Jamie asked.

"Hundreds," Grandma laughed. "Sarah, that's a very smart idea. We'll do it."

Sarah blushed proudly, and then she realized that she was starving. "Whew—now I can eat," she said. "Pass the jam, please."

*   *   *

The next morning there was a message on its way to the Israeli newspapers.

> To the daughter of Otto Schwartz, who lived in Prague, Czechoslovakia, before World War Two, or to anybody else who knew him—please write to Jamie, Sarah, and Mrs. Shirley Klein, 44 Ash Lane, Wicksville, New York, U.S.A. We are looking for information about Otto Schwartz and his coin collection.

One month later two letters from Israel reached Grandma's house. The return address of the smaller envelope read "Lisa Schwartz Marom." The larger one had the name "Yisrael Fliegel." Grandma's hands shook with excitement as she opened the larger envelope. Out fell a coin! She rushed to the phone and called Jamie and Sarah. "Drop everything, even homework, and come right over! We may have the answer to our mystery."

There were two letters in the envelope that held the coin. One was dated 1988 and signed "Yisrael Fliegel." The other was written on brittle, yellow paper and was dated 1946. It began with "Dear Srulik" and was signed "Your friend, Itzik."

"Yikes!" Jamie cried, "Itzik was Otto—our Uncle Otto!"

Sarah bounced up and down and clapped her hands, too excited to speak.

"Let's keep cool," Grandma said as she put her glasses on upside down, switched them, and finally began to read the first letter aloud.

> Dear Jamie, Sarah, and Mrs. Shirley Klein,
>
> I was a close friend of Otto Schwartz from the time we were both young boys in Hashvata, Russia. Before the First World War, I came to Palestine and Otto went to Czechoslovakia, but we continued to write to each other. In 1938 he wrote asking me to find his daughter, Lisa, who had come to Palestine. I discovered, to my sorrow, that she had been brought to Palestine on an illegal ship. When the British tried to capture the ship, she jumped overboard and drowned. Her body was identified by the papers in her pocket. Soon after I sent this tragic news to Itzik—or Otto—the Second World War broke out. I did not hear from him again until after the war. In 1946 he wrote to me again and enclosed a coin. I am sending his letter and coin because I hope they will be of use to you. I never heard from Itzik again.
>
> Sincerely,
> Yisrael Fliegel

"But Lisa didn't drown! She just wrote us this letter," Jamie protested.

Grandma chewed her thumbnail thoughtfully. She was too nervous to get herself a bagel. "You're right," she said finally. "Somebody made a terrible mistake on the day Lisa's ship came to Palestine. Maybe another girl was drowned. And maybe, in the excitement, her body was identified as Lisa's."

Jamie reached eagerly for the second letter. "Let's look at Uncle Otto's letter," he said, "and then we'll read Lisa's letter."

"Wait!" Sarah put her hand over the yellowing paper. "Please, let's identify the coin first. It's our last coin. If Uncle Otto sent it to Yisrael, then there must be something very important about it."

"Sarah, you are so mushy," Jamie grumbled. But he put down the letter and lifted the big coin book off the shelf. "Got it!" he yelled a few minutes later. "It's a silver two-zlote from Poland."

CHAPTER
17

SILVER TWO-ZLOTE, 1936
Coined in Warsaw, Poland. On one side there
is an eagle and the date. The other side shows
a three-masted sailing ship and the words "2
zlote."

"Poland, 1936," Grandma repeated. She shivered. "This coin could
have a sad story to tell. Three and a half million Jews lived in Poland
before World War Two. It was a lively community with writers, actors,
musicians, political and religious leaders, and many schools, theaters,
and other institutions. But they suffered terrible persecution. During the
war the Nazis conquered Poland and began to murder Polish Jews. By
1946, when the war ended, most of the three and a half million had been
destroyed in the Holocaust."

Grandma touched the coin and then quickly pulled back her finger as
though it burned. "It was the most terrible time in Jewish history," she
said softly.

"Worse than when the Temple was burned down?" Sarah asked.

"Worse than when the Jews were expelled from Spain?" asked Jamie.

Grandma slowly shook her head. "How can we compare 'worsts'?" she
asked. "For me this was the worst because it happened during my lifetime."

Kaddish

Poland, 1943

Berelleh was squeezed against his father's rough, black coat. He held his sister's small hand, and she held their mother's as they walked in the center of the crowd of hurrying Jews. German soldiers stood at the sides of the village street, barking orders, holding whips. And the people at the outside kept pushing to the center to get away from those whips. In the pushing, Berelleh lost his breath and stumbled, but his father's big, warm hand pulled him up. He was frightened, but his father's grip made him feel safe.

Ahead of them, at the end of the street, there were loud commands in German. The people in front began to mill around, to bounce against each other. Whips began to crack and thump. People cried out. Suddenly Berelleh's hand was wrenched from his father's. The broad back, with the ugly yellow "Jew" patch in the center, disappeared among the other black-coated, bearded men who were swept to the right. Berelleh, his sister, mother, and other women and children were driven to the left by the shouting soldiers.

"Papa!" Berelleh cried. He tried to follow the men, but his mother had picked up his sister and was pulling him along. Past the carpentry shop they went, past the mill where sunflower seeds were pressed, past the bakery still fragrant with Sabbath bread, and out along the rutted dirt road toward the ravine. Only last week he and his friend Yankel had slid into the ravine to pick berries and peek into bird's nests. Why were the Germans taking them to the ravine?

A half-circle of dusty trees stood at the edge of the ravine. The first women in the group stopped there in the shade, and the others piled into them, driven by the soldiers until they stood in a packed, confused group. Above the crowd Berelleh recognized the beautiful, curly wig of the wife of Menshel the timber merchant and the embroidered kerchief of the rebbetzin.

"Why are we here? What do you want from us?" demanded Reb Menshel's dignified wife.

"Sha, sha . . . don't get them angry. Germans don't like disorder," a quavering voice stopped her. It was their rabbi's voice. Berelleh saw him standing at the side, trembling and peering up at a black-booted German officer. Another man stood with them. He was tall and stooped, with a sandy mustache and round eyeglasses. He read from a long sheet of paper, first in Yiddish, turning to the rabbi, and then in German to the officer. His eyeglasses glinted as he looked up at the women and children and then quickly down at his paper.

When they finished reading, the officer folded the paper neatly and put it into a leather briefcase. Then he strode back, around the group of Jews, to the road. His heels thudded on the hard ridges. Soldiers with rifles followed, half-carrying the rabbi with them. Only four soldiers and the tall, sandy-haired man remained, standing close beside Berelleh's family.

Suddenly the rebbetzin cried out, "My husband, ay, my husband," and she sank to the ground. The women rushed to help her. "Give her water . . . air . . . fan her. . . ."

In the confusion, Berelleh's mother moved toward the tall man, pushing Berelleh ahead of her. She squeezed the boy's arm and whispered, "Do exactly as you are told!" Then she pulled a small pouch out of the waist of her dress. "Honored Sir," she said, speaking softly and rapidly in Yiddish to the man, "save my son—leave us a child who will say Kaddish for us," and she forced the pouch of coins down into his pocket.

The man turned pale and tried to back away. Then he made a croaking, sobbing sound. Without a word, the man pulled Berelleh back under the trees, stripped off his jacket with the yellow patch, and stuffed the ritual fringes of his shirt into his knickers. "Push your earlocks behind your ears," the man rasped in Yiddish. "Stand behind me, turn your back to the women, and don't say a word!"

Berelleh stood frozen. He jumped only once, when there was a sudden clatter, a sharp rat-tat-tat of sound from further up the ravine. The crowd stirred, questioning. The soldiers raised their guns, and one of them called out, "Our boys are chasing communists. Don't worry." The soldiers laughed. The man in front of Berelleh stood rigid as a tree.

They heard the thump of boots on the hard-packed road again. The officer and squad of soldiers returned.

"Move around the trees to the ravine!" the officer barked at the women and children. The soldiers pressed into the crowd, lashing with their whips. Children began to cry. Berelleh recognized his sister's terrified howl. He had to turn. In the crush, he saw his mother with her kerchief fallen off, her braid curling loose, and her cheek pressed against his sister Hannalleh's rosy face. His mother's brown hair mingled with the baby's golden hair

as they moved with the others around the trees to the edge of the ravine.

"What's the matter, Otto? You've no stomach for this?" The officer grinned, with a gold tooth sparkling in the sun, as he strode past them. "Think of it as sanitation . . . like killing rats."

He stopped suddenly. "Who's this?" he asked, turning Berelleh to face him.

"My nephew," the man said easily. "He lives on a farm nearby. He came to see the action."

"Ah," the officer grunted, noting Berelleh's blue eyes and light hair.

"A handsome boy. He must have Aryan blood. Keep him here, behind the trees. A child can't understand such things." He followed the soldiers to the ravine's edge.

Moments later there was a thunder of noise from beyond the trees—then silence. No babies cried. No mothers' voices soothed them. Another few scattered shots followed. Berelleh knew, deep inside, that they were shots, that all the noises had been shots, but his mind refused to think further.

Even afterwards, when the tall man lifted him into a car behind the officer, he was numb and silent. They drove through the empty village and out into the countryside. A while later the car stopped at a mud-walled farmhouse and, while the officer waited in the car, the man led him inside. He spoke earnestly to a wide-eyed peasant woman, pointed to the boy, and handed her a fistful of German marks. When the car drove off, the woman pushed Berelleh into the shed beside the house, forced him to crouch in a corner, and covered him with sacks.

In the darkness under the prickly, smelly sacks Berelleh's numbness turned into terror. "Papa, Mama, come and take me home," he sobbed, even as he knew that they couldn't come, that he was alone. "I want to be with you. Why did you make me live?"

Autumn passed, and the slow, bitter days of winter arrived. Berelleh ate dry bread, potato peels, and kashe. He drank melted snow and warmed himself against the bodies of the pigs and goats in the shed. Sometimes he sang the Kaddish softly, through stiff lips. "Yitgadal veyitkadash shemeh raba. . . ." But he wasn't sure whether he was singing it for his mother, his father, and his sister Hannalleh, or for himself.

The shed door was suddenly thrown open one night. Two dark shapes loomed against the blue-white of the snow-covered yard. "He's one of yours. Take him." muttered the peasant's voice. "We're afraid to hide him anymore. Someone will report us to the Germans." A rough hand reached in and hauled Berelleh out into the moonlight and pulled him to his feet.

That night Berelleh's life began again. He became part of a small band of Jews that had escaped from the Nazi killer squads and was hiding deep in the forest. The Jews came out only to buy food and weapons and to attack Germans.

By the next winter Berelleh was fifteen years old. He was growing strong and tall and no longer praying for death. He prayed instead that his aim should be true when he shot a gun or threw a bottle of explosives at the enemy and that he should escape quickly into the woods after each attack so that he could live to attack again.

But he remained silent and alone. These woods were not home, and these men and women were not his family. The part of him that used to laugh and shout and play with Hannalleh seemed to have died that day at the ravine. His world was gray. Only the Kaddish had meaning. "Yehei shemeh raba mevarach le'alam ule'almei almaya. . . ."

With his light hair and blue eyes Berelleh looked like a Polish boy. Since he was not likely to be picked up by the Germans, he was sent into the towns to buy supplies or to carry messages to other resistance groups.

One day he brought a desperate appeal from the Jews of the city of Warsaw—the Nazis had imprisoned 500,000 Jews inside the walls of a ghetto. Most of those prisoners had already been sent to death camps. The remaining few were determined to fight rather than be slaughtered helplessly. They organized a fighting group to battle the German army, and they asked for weapons, explosives, and more fighters.

The forest band huddled around the fire that night, arguing.

"It's suicide," said a veteran of many battles. "If we go to the ghetto, we'll die. If we fight in the forest, we have a chance to live."

Berelleh forced himself to speak. "We must help them. Otherwise they'll be led like cattle to the butcher—like my parents and sister." Tears filled his eyes. But the others turned their faces away and hunched up their shoulders. Berelleh rose and began to pack his things into a sack.

A few nights later Berelleh reached Warsaw. He crept through the snow-covered entrance of a tunnel that led from the Catholic cemetery, under the wall of the ghetto, and up into the cellar of a ghetto house.

He found a beehive of activity in the ghetto. From its rickety attics to its dank cellars and sewers, men, women, and children were preparing for battle. Because the Nazis controlled the streets, the imprisoned Jews broke through attic walls to make roadways in the air between the closely packed buildings. Tunnels were dug to connect the cellars of houses and to reach the web of sewers below the city. Young boys and girls crept through the rat-infested sewers to non-Jewish Warsaw. There, they bought food and weapons and carried them back.

At first Berelleh helped dig tunnels. Then he became a carrier. And, as he worked frantically with the others, he felt himself coming to life, beginning to feel and care again.

The winter snows melted and ran between the cobblestones on the ghetto streets. In the weak sunlight German soldiers hunted through the streets. In the attics and the cellars Berelleh and his friends were divided into groups that covered the ghetto. The post of each group was stocked with weapons and some food in preparation for the final battle.

It was early dawn of the day of the first seder of Passover when runners brought the news to the posts—German soldiers, tanks, and armored cars were moving into the ghetto.

Berelleh crouched at the window, watching the street. His body was tingling; his hands were sweating on the handle of his gun. Tzippy, another fighter, pressed close beside him, watching too. Her dark, curly hair brushed his shoulder. Bottles filled with gasoline were lined up beside her. These were the ghetto's anti-tank weapons.

"I feel so strong, so alive," Berelleh thought, "even happy . . . and yet I'm going to die. Maybe today."

"Are you afraid?" Tzippy asked.

Berelleh nodded.

"I am too. I'm not ready to die," she whispered. "I'm sixteen. There's so much I want to do." Her soft lips tightened. "But, since they say they must kill me, I'll fight them and die. They'll pay a price. They'll remember me!"

"Are you alone too?" Berelleh asked.

She smiled and looked at him teasingly. "No, I'm with you."

Their bodies were warm against each other in the chilly morning air. Both tightened as rumbling sounds rose from far down the street. An armored car filled with German soldiers moved slowly toward them. Then another. They were followed by a great, gray, crawling tank. A second tank rumbled half a block behind.

"Hold your fire!" ordered the Jewish unit leader.

The first car stopped in front of their building. Soldiers began to jump out.

"Fire!" he cried.

Berelleh fired again and again. "For Papa, for Mama, for Hannalleh," he heard himself screaming as he pulled the trigger. The men below spun around and stumbled; some scuttled to the car or into the houses. Beside him, Tzippy's arm swung back and out. A bottle flew at the tank and splattered. A second flew, hit, and burst into flames. Suddenly the tank was burning, with black smoke boiling out. The second tank backed up, turned clumsily like a great turtle, and rumbled back the way it had come.

Berelleh kept firing at the trucks and the men in the street while a squad of fighters raced down the steps to drive the Germans from the hallways. The armored cars screeched backward, scraped around the tank, and raced away, leaving bodies on the cobblestones.

Tzippy flung her arms around Berelleh. "We drove them off!" she cried. "The Nazi supermen ran like rabbits!" Her eyes grew wide with a sudden, impossible hope. "Maybe, maybe . . ."

"No," Berelleh shook his head, "they'll be back." But, as the group cleaned guns and prepared supplies, he found himself hoping too, silently. "Maybe we'll beat them. Maybe we'll live." For the first time since the day at the ravine he realized that he wanted very much to live.

Before noon they again heard the rumbling sound of heavy trucks. A strange khaki-colored truck, carrying a tank and hoses, led four armored cars filled with soldiers. The fighters waited with fingers on triggers or wrapped around the necks of bottles.

The truck stopped behind the blackened tank. For a moment there was a terrible, foreboding silence. Suddenly a stream of flame shot out of the truck and raced up the wall of their building. Somebody screamed. The smell of burning hair filled the room. Tzippy moved smoothly beside him . . . arm back and out. The bottles flew, and Berelleh kept firing down at the men spilling out of the trucks.

Some Nazis fell. Some crouched and aimed up at the building. Bullets began to smack against the bricks around the windows. The room was full of smoke and flames.

"Yitbarach veyishtabach veyitpaar veyitromam . . ." Berelleh recited the Kaddish as he stopped to reload. Tzippy's arm dropped, and she slipped slowly down and fell onto the window sill beside him.

"Veyitnasei veyithadar veyitaleh veyithalal . . ." Berelleh shouted the words out into the flames. Then a bullet found him also, and his body fell forward, covering the body of his friend.

• • •

Sarah carefully drew the picture of the two-zlote into the notebook. Then, at last, it was time to turn to the ancient, yellowing
pages of Uncle Otto's letter. Grandma's hand shook as she picked
them up and began to read.

Dear Srulik,
    You will be surprised to receive this letter. You proba-
bly thought I was dead. Many times during these past
six years I wished I could have died. But I had a mission
to carry out.
    Before the war began, I was asked to find a buyer
for my synagogue's valuable coin collection. The money
was needed to help our poorer members escape from
Czechoslovakia, which was already under Nazi rule. I
hid the collection, went to Switzerland where I found
a purchaser, and returned, using a false passport in a
non-Jewish name. As a non-Jew I would have more freedom to move about without being arrested. Two days
later the war broke out, and I was trapped in Czechoslovakia. It was too late to help the people of my synagogue.
I had to get out of Prague where people knew me and
might betray me to the Germans. I got a job as an inter-
preter, working with the German army, and was carried
along in the invasion of Russia.

I cannot describe the horror of the next few years. The Germans marched through town after town, pulled out all the Jewish inhabitants, and killed them on the spot or sent them to death camps. I was the miserable, cowardly witness to thousands of deaths. Only once had I the courage to risk my life, and then only because a doomed Jewish mother forced a few Polish zlotes into my pocket and shamed me into saving her young son. After the war I looked for the boy but couldn't find him. Only the zlotes remain to remind me of him.

Tomorrow I am going to dig up the coin collection. Once I treasured these coins. Each one spoke to me about its own time, about the richness of Jewish life, and the striving for godliness, for a better world, for the return to our homeland. But today, after the Holocaust, it's hard to think good thoughts. The coins are stained with blood.

Perhaps I'll sell the collection and become rich. Perhaps I'll bring it to Palestine to return it to the Jewish people. I don't know.

I am sending you one of the coins that the Jewish mother gave me as proof that I did one good thing during these terrible years. Srulik, my dear old friend, please think kindly of me.

Your friend, Itzik

Grandma took off her glasses and hunted blindly for a tissue. "Poor man," she said, "he kept all that guilt and misery locked up inside himself. Grandpa and I never knew what he had lived through."

Sarah got a tissue for Grandma and one for herself. And they all sat looking at the two-zlote and the neat handwriting on the yellowed paper.

Finally Jamie blew his nose, cleared his throat, and said, "Let's read the last letter." He tore open the small envelope. A bright, sun-filled photograph and a page of writing slipped out onto the table.

"This will be a happier letter, Grandma," said Sarah. She patted her grandmother's hand. "See—all the people in the picture look happy."

Grandma nodded. She rubbed her eyes and put her glasses back on. "Read, Jamie," she said.

Dear Mrs. Shirley Klein, Jamie, and Sarah,
    How exciting to see your ad asking about Otto Schwartz.
    Otto Schwartz was my father! He owned a large department store in Prague and was the caretaker of his synagogue's valuable coin collection. I was an only child.

My mother died when I was a baby. I lived with Papa until I was sixteen. In 1938, against my father's wishes, I left home and came to Palestine as an illegal immigrant. I wrote to him from Palestine, but all my letters were returned.

When the war ended, I searched through all the records of the agencies that helped survivors of the Holocaust and collected the names of those who had been killed. There was no trace of Otto Schwartz. Finally I forced myself to realize that he had died or been killed during the war and was buried without a name, like so many of our people.

I loved him very much and still feel sad that we parted angrily. But I am very happy that I came to Palestine and that I have raised my family in the State of Israel. My son, Yitzhak, is named after Papa. He is a tall, sandy-haired man with a wide, blond mustache. He looks so much like my father, Otto. And my daughter is named Hildy after a dear friend who died before she could reach Palestine.

My husband Levi and I live in a kibbutz near the city of Haifa. We have fish ponds, peach trees, a basketball court, and a swimming pool. Please come to visit us. I'm sure that Jamie and Sarah would enjoy meeting our seven grandchildren. I would love to share any information you have about my father.

Le'hitra'ot [see you soon]!

Lisa Schwartz Marom

P.S. I enclose a picture of my family. I am sitting in the middle holding our youngest grandchild. Yitzhak is standing behind me. And Hildy is behind Levi.

Jamie put down the letter and grinned at Sarah and Grandma. "We did it!" he exclaimed. "We finally have an explanation of Uncle Otto's coin collection."

"We know why he called it 'blood money,'" said Grandma.

"And we know why he wouldn't talk about it. He was so sad and ashamed," said Sarah. "Now I wish we could write a happy ending, like . . . the wicked fairy disappeared in a puff of smoke and the prince and princess lived happily ever after."

"Lisa's letter is a kind of happy ending," Jamie suggested. "It's very sad because of the Holocaust and Hildy and Uncle Otto, but it's happy too because of Lisa and Israel."

"Yes, it's happy," Grandma said firmly, as if she was trying to convince herself.

Sarah breathed a satisfied sigh. "This letter sounded so happy. I feel better now."

"I do too," said Jamie. "Grandma, let's go and visit them. With seven grandchildren, some of them are sure to be the same age as Sarah and me."

Grandma clapped her hands at a sudden thought. "We have to do more than visit. We have to introduce Lisa to Srulik. Maybe Srulik has some great-grandchildren for you to meet. But, most important of all, we must bring Uncle Otto's coin collection to the Israel Museum. Then it will belong to the whole Jewish people, just as he wanted."

"I'll miss it," Sarah said. She ran her fingers over the coins in the bowl.

"Then we'll have to visit it often," Jamie said. "Uh-oh, we'd better start practicing Hebrew." He reached out and shook Grandma's hand enthusiastically. "Shalom, Savta. Ani Jamie. He Sarah. Le'hitra'ot!"

Sources

Carson, R. A. *Coins of the World: Ancient, Medieval, Modern.* New York: Harper and Row, 1962.
Chapter   3: Gold Stater, plate 1, #2
           6: Bronze Denari, plate 20, #295
           7: Gold Dinar, plate 54, #876
           8: Silver Dirhem, plate 54, #877
           9: Bronze Chien, plate 61, #1001
          10: Golden Sequin, #903
          11: Gold Coin, #841
          12: Copper Groschen, #699
          13: Zolota, #905
          14: Gold Ducat
          15: Silver Piaster

Coins Reveal. Samuel and Daniel M. Friedenberg collection of coins and medals. New York: Jewish Museum, 1983.
Chapter   4: Bronze Coin, page 14, #14
          5: Bronze Half-Shekel, page 29, #66

National Geographic, December 1982, page 759.
Chapter   1: Golden-Headed Horse

Yeoman, R. S. *A Catalog of Modern World Coins.* New York: Western Publishing Co., Inc. (Golden Press), 1979.
Chapter 16: Bronze One Mil
Chapter 17: Silver Two-Zlote

About the Author/Illustrator

Chaya M. Burstein is the author/illustrator of many books for children, including *Rifka Grows Up* and *The Jewish Kids Catalog*, winners of the National Jewish Book Award for children's literature. She writes about herself: "I was brought up with Bible stories and shtetl stories rather than with tales of Mother Goose. The goats and chickens of my mother's small town in Russia became imaginary friends. And Sarah, Deborah the Judge, and King Solomon felt like an extended family. I would sit on the milk box in front of my family's grocery store in Brooklyn writing stories and drawing paper dolls. There wasn't much time for writing and drawing as I grew older. I worked as a draftswoman, married, lived on a kibbutz in Israel, returned to America, and had three children. But the old stories were still tucked away in my mind. Finally, I took a course in illustration at the School of Visual Arts in New York and got to work on *Rifka Bangs the Teakettle*, a story about my mother's village. Seven other books have followed. When I'm not writing or drawing pictures, I enjoy hiking, canoeing, and making 'connect-the-dots' pictures for my grandchildren."